a batch
made in
heaven

Also by Suzanne Nelson

a batch
made in
heaven

Suzanne Nelson

SCHOLASTIC INC.

Copyright © 2021 by Suzanne Nelson

All rights reserved. Published by Scholastic Inc., *Publishers since 1920*.

SCHOLASTIC and associated logos are trademarks and/or registered trademarks of Scholastic Inc.

The publisher does not have any control over and does not assume any responsibility for author or third-party websites or their content.

No part of this publication may be reproduced, stored in a retrieval system, or transmitted in any form or by any means, electronic, mechanical, photocopying, recording, or otherwise, without written permission of the publisher. For information regarding permission, write to Scholastic Inc., Attention: Permissions Department, 557 Broadway, New York, NY 10012.

This book is a work of fiction. Names, characters, places, and incidents are either the product of the author's imagination or are used fictitiously, and any resemblance to actual persons, living or dead, business establishments, events, or locales is entirely coincidental.

Library of Congress Cataloging-in-Publication Data available

ISBN 978-1-338-64050-2

10 9 8 7 6 5 4 3 2 1   21 22 23 24 25

Printed in the U.S.A.   40
First printing 2021
Book design by Jennifer Rinaldi

For librarians and
educators everywhere.
Thank you for nourishing young
minds with delicious books,
now and always.

—S.N.

Chapter One

I stood outside Mr. Imari's social studies class, an electric excitement humming beneath my skin. I was wearing my Ruth Bader Ginsburg T-shirt that read WOMEN BELONG IN ALL PLACES WHERE DECISIONS ARE BEING MADE. It was my favorite out of the many "power tees" I owned. I had some with phrases like ACTIONS, NOT WORDS or TRY ME, but I wore this particular one on days when I felt like I could conquer the world.

"Mina, how are you not more nervous?" my best friend, Kalliah Edmiston, asked me, pressing a quivering palm against her forehead. "Ugh, I feel nauseous."

I glanced down at the image of RBG on my shirt. "Come on, Kalli. Just think . . . what would Ruth do?"

Kalli grimaced. "Not stress, I know. But I can't help it."

I gave her a smile, hoping my positive energy might boost hers. Her crinkled brow and puckered lips told me that didn't seem likely.

Kalli and I both had big brown eyes and thick black hair, although she wore hers down to her waist, and I kept mine shorter, to my shoulders. Kalli's olive skin was several shades lighter than my dark brown skin. And personality-wise, we were nothing alike; I often joked that Kalli was the Eeyore to my Pooh. A member of the Oyster Cove Middle School Honor Society, student council, and half a dozen community service organizations, Kalli was a straight-A student and massive over-achiever, but she was also a chronic worrier. If she could only get more comfortable with extroverting, she could totally be president of the United States someday.

"Remember how excited we were to do this?" I reminded Kalli. She nodded weakly.

I thought back to two weeks ago, when Mr. Imari had first told our class about the new seventh-grade mentorship program. A few local business owners had each agreed to take on a youth mentee for the month of October to help them learn the ins and outs of some of our town's independently owned businesses. Kalli and I had skimmed the list of participating businesses together, and she'd instantly homed in on the docent's apprentice job at the Oyster Cove History Museum.

"I'd love to work on their exhibit on the Native American tribes of Washington State," she'd said determinedly. Kalli is descended from the Chinookan people on her mother's side. Her family moved to Oyster Cove years ago, but most of her mom's relatives still lived along the Columbia River. "It'd be so great for the museum to have more information about the Chinook and the Samish, especially since this region is home to the Samish Indian Nation."

"That would be awesome," I'd said.

Then I'd looked back at the list and nearly shrieked when I saw A Batch Made in Heaven, with *Baker's Apprentice* written beside it. Specializing in inventive and delicious cookies, A Batch Made in Heaven was my favorite "foodie" spot in all of Oyster Cove. Baking was my passion and something that I'd grown up doing with my dad. He'd owned a restaurant in Delhi, India, before my mom had gotten her scholarship to study molecular biology at Washington State University. When he and my mom immigrated to America and had me, Dad had had to leave his restaurant behind. Maybe to distract himself from the loss of the restaurant, he'd decided to learn a new skill: baking. Even better, he'd shared it with me. And now I had the chance to be an official baker's apprentice.

"Omigod!" I'd latched on to Kalli's arm. "That's it! That one's mine!"

"No surprise there, Bakerella." Kalli had laughed. "That job was made for you and your spatula. I can't believe Batch is actually participating. Aren't Mr. Winston's recipes top secret?"

"Yeah, that's the story, but that doesn't mean he can't have an apprentice." I imagined working alongside Mr. Winston, the idiosyncratic owner of A Batch Made in Heaven. "How amazing would it be if he confided all of his baking tips to me? That would be like striking culinary gold. Maybe he's ready to share his recipes?"

A Batch Made in Heaven was steeped in local lore. People had been known to make the two-hour drive north from Seattle to our small, picturesque harbor town just to pick up a dozen freshly baked Batch cookies. Sometimes, visitors came from farther afield, stopping into Batch during road trips or vacations so that they could brag on social media about tasting the famous cookies.

Mr. Winston had achieved near-celeb status himself. Rumor had it that he was notoriously demanding with the bakery's hand-selected employees, making them sign confidentiality agreements so that none of them would ever reveal any of his baking secrets. Sometimes he was known to yell in Gordon Ramsay fashion at his employees.

But I wasn't worried about working for someone moody. Every

genius has their quirks, and what he lacked in good temper his cookies made up for in taste. Mr. Winston invented the best cookie recipes *ever*, and learning from him would make me a better baker.

So when Mr. Imari told us to submit our top three choices for mentor positions, the baking job was at the top of my list, highlighted and underlined (twice for extra emphasis). Even so, writing down alternate choices made me uneasy. The whole process felt a little bit like pulling a random Career card in the board game Life. That was my least favorite part of the Life game—not having the power to choose my own path.

This morning, awaiting our mentorship assignments, I refused to even consider the possibility that I might not get the job of my dreams.

"I'd be calmer," Kalli was telling me now as we stood outside the classroom, "if I knew for sure I was getting the job at the museum. But what if I don't? What if I have to be an apprentice . . . on the Oyster Cove Ferry?"

She shivered, and I stifled a laugh as her cheeks took on a

green cast. Being out on the water of Puget Sound ranked among Kalli's top nightmare scenarios.

Back in the third grade, when Kalli and I had first become friends, my dad and I had taken her out on our sailing skiff, the *Akshiti*. Within fifteen minutes, Kalli was so seasick we had to turn the skiff back toward shore. She'd sworn never to set foot on a boat again.

"Hey, you'd be the picture of fashion in your life jacket, even hanging over the side of the ferry the whole time," I teased playfully. She didn't crack a smile. "But you're *going* to get the job at the museum, and I'm *going* to get the job at A Batch Made in Heaven. And it will be amazing." I tried to hold back a yawn, but it was unstoppable. "*If* I can stay awake."

Kalli offered me a sympathetic glance. "The twins were up all night again?"

I nodded with a sigh. My new brother and sister, Amul and Banita, were only twelve weeks old, but it felt like they'd been crying for centuries. Their nursery shared a wall with my bedroom, which made it impossible for me to sleep through their nightly outbursts.

"I remember how happy you were when you found out your mom was pregnant," Kalli said. "You couldn't wait to be a big sister. You hated being an only child."

"True." I'd resigned myself to being an only child years ago, mostly because whenever I'd asked for a little brother or sister, Mom and Dad had responded with an adamant no. Then my parents found out they were having the twins, who were, as Mom put it, "double the surprise for double the fun."

"And I do love the twins," I said to Kalli now. "*So* much." I thought of their warm, sleepy cuddliness when I gave them bottles, the downy-soft black curls sprouting in tiny tufts on the crowns of their heads. A pang of missing them hit me. "But they cry *all* the time. I'm too tired to try out any new recipes. Last night, I tried to make a batch of nankhatais . . ."

"Yuummmm." Kalli closed her eyes dreamily. She loved my nankhatais because I used extra ghee and cardamom for a slightly more citrusy, softer cookie. "Did you bring some for me?"

I shook my head. "I ended up having to help my mom with Amul and Banita. I forgot about the cookies and . . . poof!" I made an exploding gesture with my hands. "Cookie inferno. Burnt to a crisp."

"Oh no." Kalli clutched her chest in sympathy. "That's painful."

"Tell me about it. The twins are awesome. It's just . . . hard." That word didn't even come close to quantifying the amount of upheaval in my family, but I was too tired to come up with a better one. "But this mentorship is going to get me out of the house once a week for a whole month!" I fist-pumped the air in celebration, finally able to get a laugh out of Kalli.

"I guess *any* job has to be better than changing diapers." She wrinkled her nose.

"So. True," I said, giggling. "See? That's definitely a positive! Attagirl. Keep going," I prodded gently.

"And," Kalli went on as we walked into the classroom and took our seats, "it's not like this is what we'll be doing for the rest of our lives. Mr. Imari said this is just a job 'tasting' so we can get the flavor of it."

From all around us came excited chatter as our classmates speculated on what type of "job" they'd get.

"I've always wanted to ride in a fire truck with sirens blaring," José Alvarez was saying wistfully, while Sara Brightman was gushing about the possibility of working at Bead-azzle, our town's DIY jewelry-making store. It was obvious that Kalli and I weren't the only ones who had our hearts set on specific jobs.

The chatter died down after the bell rang, and Mr. Imari began handing out the mentorship assignments. As he approached our desks, I locked eyes with Kalli and clasped her hand, giving it an affirming squeeze.

"Here we go," I whispered as Mr. Imari placed our assignments facedown on our desks.

I counted to three, and we flipped our papers over.

"Yes!" we whisper-shrieked at the same time.

The words *Baker's Apprentice* blazed beautifully up at me from my page. And Kalli's paper read *Docent's Apprentice*. Just as I'd predicted! We grinned at each other.

I twisted around to see our friends Jane and Fabiana at their desks. They gave me and Kalli excited thumbs-up signs. That meant they'd gotten *their* dream jobs at the Bookworm. I'd been worried that our small local bookstore might only have enough room for one apprentice, and I was glad they'd both been accepted. Based on the squeals around us, it seemed that most people had gotten their first choice, though there were a few groans of disappointment mixed in, too.

Mr. Imari was going over the rules for expected behavior during our mentorships, but my head spun with visions of gleaming stainless-steel ovens and rolling baking racks with their sleek wheels. Best of all, I imagined the peace permeating the kitchen. It would be free of wailing babies, baskets of dirty laundry, and bottles waiting to be sterilized. Working at A Batch Made in Heaven was going to be perfect.

I was still grinning when Kalli and I walked to the cafeteria for lunch. As we got into the long lunch line, Kalli's fingers flew over her phone's screen.

"I'm texting my mom right now to see if we can ask my

grandma to loan us some artifacts for the exhibit. Maybe she'll even let me wear some of our ancestors' Chinook clothing when I'm helping with tours at the museum."

"That would be so cool."

As I set a cup of fruit salad on my tray, the words "mentor program" drifted down the lunch line, catching my ear. I peered around, searching for a face to go with the voice.

Finally, my eyes settled on Flynn Winston. He was in eighth grade, a year ahead of Kalli and me. His curly dark-auburn hair, striking indigo eyes, and tall, lanky stature made him easy to spot at our school. I had a hard time *not* noticing Flynn in general. It wasn't just that he was cute (okay, *very* cute). He was the son of Mr. Winston—as in the owner of A Batch Made in Heaven. He often worked at Batch after school, ringing up customers at the sales counter.

As I watched Flynn now, I imagined us working together. He'd be showing me how to work the cash register, and I'd instantly be a pro. Then he'd smile at me, and our shoulders would brush, and—

"I can't believe I have to put up with some seventh grader." Flynn's words were loud enough to jar me from my daydream, and I homed in on the conversation he was having with a boy named Trent, who was captain of the archery team. "I don't get why my dad even agreed to have an apprentice in the first place."

Trent shrugged. "Seems like most of the businesses in town are participating. And maybe your dad needs a break. The shop sells an unbelievable amount of cookies."

"My dad needs a break? *That's* funny." Flynn's laugh was tinged with bitterness. "Besides, we're busy enough without throwing some newbie into the mix."

I bristled at the word "newbie." How *dare* he? He was talking about me like I was some toddler just off the playground! The humiliation of it stung. I nudged Kalli and jerked my head in Flynn's direction. She nodded, to let me know she was hearing his words, too.

"Who's he calling 'newbie'?" I hissed. Kalli's eyes widened with worry. She knew me so well, she guessed (rightly) that it was only a matter of seconds before I spoke up to defend myself.

"Mina," she whispered pleadingly with me. "Just let it go—"

"Shh." I held up a finger for quiet as Trent and Flynn started talking again.

"It's only for a few weeks," Trent said to Flynn. "How bad could it be?"

Flynn shook his head. "All I know is that my dad better not expect me to babysit somebody who can't tell a spatula from a spoon."

My back stiffened. *"Rude!"* I whispered to Kalli. Heat flashed over my face, and my hands held my lunch tray in a vise grip. Then, despite Kalli's quiet imploring, I marched toward Flynn.

When I tapped him on the shoulder, he spun around and looked momentarily surprised. My breath caught, because I'd never actually been this close to him before. Now that there wasn't a sales counter between us, I could see the lighter flecks of aqua in his indigo irises, and—oh *wow*—were his eyes amazing. For a split second, I couldn't think clearly. But then his words came back to me, and I regained my senses.

"Hi," I said curtly. "I'm Mina Kapur, the new apprentice at A Batch Made in Heaven." I waited for that to sink in, watching with some satisfaction as redness swept over his fair, freckled cheeks. "Sorry to disappoint you, but I won't be needing any babysitting. I've been baking all my life, so you might learn a thing or two from *me*." I held up my hand in a cheery wave and swiveled on my heel, calling over my shoulder, "See you at the shop after school!"

Kalli's mouth was gaping as she steered me toward our table. "I can't believe you did that!" she whispered, both stunned and impressed.

"I had to!" Then the boldness of what I'd said to Flynn hit me, and I sank weakly onto the lunch bench. "Omigod, did I really just tell off the cutest guy in school?"

Kalli giggled and looked horrified all at once. "You did."

I raised my chin. "Well . . . good. There was no way I could stay silent with him being so . . . so condescending."

"To be fair," Kalli pointed out, "he didn't know you were

standing behind him. And I'm sure he didn't know you were the one who got the mentorship."

I frowned. "I guess . . . And the strange thing is, Flynn never seemed like a jerk before. Maybe he's just having a bad day?"

"Could be," Kalli offered with her typical leniency. "Honestly, I'm not sure anybody really *knows* Flynn."

It was true. There was something mysterious about Flynn. Aside from Trent and Will, his two best buds, Flynn mostly kept to himself. His name was always on the school's honor roll, and from the books I often saw him reading during lunch, I guessed he was both smart and driven. But I rarely saw him joking around and roughhousing the way some of the other boys did. At the bakery, he always seemed polite and efficient, but behind his smile was a thinly veiled frustration. Now I wondered why.

I groaned as a new worry struck me. "What if he's awful to work with?"

Kalli popped an orange slice into her mouth. "Mina, you're a force of nature. He'll see that soon enough and be grateful for your help."

I smiled. "Thanks. I hope we can just start fresh at the shop after school."

"That's a perfect plan. A clean slate, a cute boy, and . . ."

"Cookies!" We finished the sentence together, and then broke into laughter.

I smiled at Kalli. "What could possibly go wrong?"

Chapter Two

Three hours later, Kalli and I walked down Main Street on our way to our respective mentorships. Kalli was going to drop me off at Batch first and then head on to the museum. We'd already dropped off Jane and Fabs at the Bookworm.

October had arrived in Oyster Cove the way it had for most of northwestern Washington State—with clouds and chilly rain. Today, though, the sky was a cloudless, brilliant blue and a crisp breeze was blowing in from Puget Sound. I could see the majestic blue silhouettes of the distant North Cascade mountains. To our west, the bay was dotted with the crisp white sails of boats out for a ride around the San Juan Islands. To the east, people lounged on their sun-soaked decks, taking in the water views and warm weather. The rare sunshine had drawn most people out into our quaint downtown for strolls and shopping.

My heart jumped when the robin's-egg-blue awning of A Batch Made in Heaven came into view. Printed on the awning was the bakery's famous logo: a plate of haloed cookies floating on a fluffy white cloud. Kalli and I stopped outside the bakery, and we breathed in the deliciously sweet aroma of hot-out-of-the-oven cookies.

"I don't see why Mr. Winston even bothers advertising," Kalli said. "His cookies come with their own built-in marketing plan. One sniff and you're sold."

I nodded with a grin. "And just think—I'll get to taste-test the cookies before anyone else. As my BFF, you'll have VIP cookie-tasting status, too. I'll make sure of it."

Worry flicked over Kalli's face. "Won't that get you in trouble? Giving freebies out to friends?"

I nudged Kalli. "When are you going to quit worrying so much?"

"Um . . . never?" She laughed quietly. "I'm the worrier. You're the warrior. We balance each other out." Her eyes wandered toward the shop's window, and her smile fell. "Uh-oh." She leaned toward me and whispered, "Don't look now, but Flynn's working at the counter. He spotted you, and . . ." She squirmed uncomfortably. "He doesn't exactly seem happy to see you."

My adrenaline surged, and I tried not to look. "Why? What's he doing?"

Kalli pressed her lips together. "Staring. And it's hard to tell, but I think glaring, too?" She gazed at me in concern. "Sorry."

Since my run-in with Flynn at lunch, I'd commanded myself to stay levelheaded. I was focused, rational Mina Kapur, a girl on a mission to become a world-renowned baker. I wouldn't let Flynn distract me from that mission.

But the second I peeked through the window and spotted Flynn, all my convictions melted quick as butter.

"You'll be okay," Kalli told me, squeezing my hand, in a definite role reversal.

I swallowed my nerves and gave her a big smile to show her I was *more* than okay. Whenever Kalli, Jane, or Fabiana had a problem, they came to me for solutions. I was the one who talked them through fights with parents, or failed tests, or whatever the drama of the day was. I liked being my friends' shoulder to lean on. Lately, I'd mastered that same confident smile around my parents. My smile said they didn't need to worry about me, especially now that they had the new babies to worry over.

"Of course I will," I told Kalli, feigning nonchalance. "Once Flynn sees my baking skills, he'll drop whatever attitude he has."

Kalli nodded, then checked her watch. "I've got to get over to the museum." She gave me a quick hug. "Good luck!"

"You too." I waved as she turned to walk the two blocks to the museum. Then I set my shoulders and walked into the shop, head held high.

A Batch Made in Heaven was packed. Every chair was occupied, including the swivel stools at the counter. A line of customers stood reading the menu board on the wall and discussing what to order. I wondered which cookie I'd get to bake first. Kalli's fave was the Sweet 'n' Salty, which was made with three different kinds of caramel and toffee bits, marshmallows, pretzels, and sea salt. Then there was the Candy Bar Crush, made with five different types of candy bars. But my absolute favorite was the Cookie Monster, an everything-but-the-kitchen-sink cookie that was full of pretzels, potato chips, and chocolate morsels.

I wove around the customers, and my mouth watered as I passed Vera Hernandez, one of my classmates. She was pulling apart a gooey Fabulous Fudge cookie to reveal its brownie-stuffed center.

I glanced at Flynn, who was ringing up customers at the counter, expecting him to offer me a hello or at least point me in the direction of his dad. When he did neither, disappointment pricked my insides, but then I straightened with resolve.

Fine, I thought, *I can find him myself.*

I heard Mr. Winston before I saw him. His voice boomed from behind the door of the shop's kitchen, and from the sound of it, he wasn't happy.

The Cookie Vault was the nickname for Mr. Winston's

kitchen. The Vault was rumored to be so top secret that hardly anyone besides Mr. Winston was ever allowed inside. I hoped that wasn't true, because I'd already made it my own personal goal to bake inside the Vault.

Now the Vault's door burst open, and Mr. Winston's six-foot-three, broad-shouldered figure filled its frame. He was wearing his signature duckbill hat and chef's coat, which was white with blue piping and had the Batch Made in Heaven logo embroidered over the breast pocket. He carried a silver tray laden with cookies.

"Where's Hughie?" Mr. Winston demanded of Flynn.

Flynn shrugged, nonplussed by his dad's scowl. "Not out here" came his flat response.

Mr. Winston groaned. "He forgot to set the timer. Again! The latest cookies are dry as bricks!"

I guessed Hughie was one of the shop's small troop of employees. Mr. Winston was known for keeping the staff to a bare minimum, and the people he hired sometimes only lasted a week or two before quitting or getting fired. This fact might've scared away other seventh graders, but not me. I wasn't planning on giving Mr. Winston any reason to be unhappy with my job performance. I was going to be a perfect apprentice. Starting right now.

"Mr. Winston." I waved cheerfully. "I can help. Pour some espresso or ganache over bits of the cookies, then add a scoop of ice cream. They'll taste just as fantastic. Or you can stick them in a cookie jar with the heel of a loaf of bread." Out of the corner of my eye, I noticed customers staring at me openmouthed, shocked that I was actually daring to give Mr. Winston, the Cookie King himself, advice about cookies. I kept my smile glued to my face. "My dad taught me that trick when I was little. The cookies will moisten right up."

I hoped Mr. Winston would thank me or break into a relieved smile. Instead, he stared at me blankly. "Who are you?"

"Mina Kapur," I replied. Still the blank stare. "I'm your seventh-grade apprentice from Oyster Cove Middle School?"

I waited through a long, uncomfortable pause, and then, at last, he grunted. "Oh. Right." His eyes flicked toward a harried-looking man in an apron who'd emerged from the small office at the back of the store. He had a cell phone in one hand and his laptop under his arm. "Hughie." Mr. Winston's voice was low but loaded with exasperation.

Hughie hurried toward Mr. Winston, gushing apologies. "I needed to make a phone call, and—"

"We don't have time for excuses." Mr. Winston cut him off.

"No, of course not." Hughie opened the calendar app on his phone. "You have that podcast recording for *Dessert Daily* in ten minutes . . ."

"And we haven't done the social media posting for the day," Mr. Winston said.

"I'm on it." Hughie caught sight of me, and relief swept across his face. "Oh, Mina, thank goodness you're here!" I blinked in confusion but didn't have a chance to ask how *he* knew who I was. "Do we *ever* need your help."

I resurrected my smile. "I'm thrilled to be here. Baking is my passion, and I especially love cookies—"

"Yes, yes, I read all about that on your application. It's why I decided you were a shoo-in. But more importantly, how are you with social media?"

"Oh. Pretty good!" I said enthusiastically. The truth was, I wasn't allowed to have an Instagram account yet (my parents said I had to wait until I was thirteen), but I knew enough about it from people who did have accounts, like my friend Jane. Still, I didn't get how social media had anything to do with my baking skills. "Wait. Did you say . . . *you* decided I was a shoo-in?" My mind whirred, trying to make sense of it all. "But didn't Mr. Winston—"

Hughie shook his head. "Mr. Winston is far too busy inventing recipes for this sort of everyday minutia." Hughie turned to face the customers in line and called out, "Hi, everyone! Who wants to be in the Smart Cookie post today?" A slew of hands shot into the air, and a few kids actually squealed with excitement. Hughie scrutinized the expectant faces. "You, you . . ." He pointed. "And you."

He flew into action, quickly positioning the chosen kids

around Mr. Winston, whose entire demeanor transformed from annoyed to enthusiastic in record time. With the air of a person who knew his most photogenic side, Mr. Winston raised the cookie-laden silver tray above his head like he was lifting a barbell. The fans surrounding him all raised cookies to their lips as Hughie snapped pics with his phone.

"Thanks, all!" Hughie said, and as soon as he did, Mr. Winston set down the tray and disappeared into the kitchen. Hughie, meanwhile, swiped through the pics on his screen and nodded in approval. "As long as it's okay with your parents," he told the kids, "I'll tag you all when I post the pic. Help yourselves to another cookie, on the house."

The group happily emptied the platter of cookies in record time.

Hughie took a seat at a free table and motioned for me to join him. "Mina, here comes your crash course in Cookie Commerce 101," he said, handing me his phone.

I took a seat, unsure what to do with the phone. Hughie flipped open his laptop and began typing away as some spreadsheets filled the screen. My gaze found its way back to the kitchen door. "I'm looking forward to working with Mr. Winston," I said hopefully. "I've never baked anything in an industrial kitchen before, but I'm a fast learner and I—"

"Love baking *and* cookies. I know." Hughie's fingers paused over the keys long enough for him to actually make eye contact with me, and he offered me a genuine, if somewhat pitying, smile. "Those are not *now* issues. The *now* issue is that business is booming, and I can't keep up with the cookie volume *and* the shop's social media." He gestured to the phone in my hand. "Look at the pics I took, choose the best one, add a good filter, and post it to the shop's IG feed. You'll see the captions and hashtags we use in the other Smart Cookie posts, so you can just borrow from that . . ."

"You want me to choose the picture?" I asked. So far, none of what he'd said had anything to do with baking cookies.

"Yes! Our followers will love whatever you post," Hughie said, turning back to his laptop. "And next, please take and post a picture of the Oreo Rodeo—the Cookie of the Day."

I glanced down at Hughie's phone, my mind reeling. I didn't want to start my first day on the job by being argumentative, but at the same time, I had to *say* something. "After I'm done with the photos, I'll be baking with Mr. Winston, right? Because this *is* a baking mentorship."

Hughie tilted his head at me and sighed. "Mina, I wish I could tell you that this apprenticeship was all about baking. But baking isn't where we need the help. Branding is. This is about learning what it takes to run a successful business. Brand image and social networking are two of Mr. Winston's top priorities. And he has strict standards when it comes to who gains his confidence. Earning it will take some time."

"Oh." I dropped my gaze, my cheeks griddle-hot with mortification. "That makes sense." I was a big believer in self-advocating, but I didn't want Hughie to misread my questions as ingratitude. "I'm excited to learn about every part of the business."

"Good." Hughie gave me a friendly, reassuring smile, then closed his laptop and jumped up. "I've got to get back to the kitchen now. Don't forget to post the pics!"

*　　*　　*

Half an hour later, I'd posted everything to social media and earned the praise of Hughie.

"Very well-written," he said, reading through the IG posts on his phone. "You did a wonderful job with the filters, too. The Oreo Rodeo looks amazing."

"Thanks." Still, I couldn't quell my disappointment that he was the one reviewing my work instead of Mr. Winston.

Hughie pocketed his phone. "Why don't you check in with Flynn to see if he needs any help behind the counter?" he said. "I've got to do a quick inventory review."

"Great!" I jumped at the chance to shadow Flynn as he worked. Finally, I could prove to him that I was no "newbie."

I hovered at the counter's edge, waiting for Flynn to motion me through the flip-up counter door. I caught his sideways glance in my direction, but he made no move to welcome me through. Fresh anger heated my insides. The very least he should have done was offer me an apology for his earlier rudeness. I flipped up the door and walked determinedly over to him.

"I'm here to help," I said matter-of-factly.

"I don't need any help." His voice was flat as he handed a bag of cookies to the waiting customer. The butter in the cookies was already dimpling the blue bag—evidence of their excessive richness. "It's under control."

I nearly scoffed. I was starting to get the impression that control was something he liked.

He gave me the briefest glance, but when he did, his eyes disarmed me again. They were the color of the bay at dusk.

I lost my train of thought but then forced myself to recover before I showed any sign of being flustered. "Look"—I offered him a reconciliatory smile—"we got off on the wrong foot earlier. Obviously, you're not thrilled about this situation. But I'm working here for the next month, so maybe we can call a truce?"

He opened his mouth to say something, then snapped it shut again. Instead of answering me, he turned to face the next customer.

I glanced around, searching for something I could help with. If he wouldn't give me a job, I'd find one myself.

At last, I spotted a napkin dispenser on the counter that was nearly empty, and within seconds, I was refilling it with a store of napkins I discovered on a lower shelf. Next, I organized cookie boxes by size. Determined not to give in to Flynn's standoffishness, I occasionally struck up one-sided conversations, hoping he'd eventually respond.

"The Oreo Rodeo seems to be selling the best of all the cookies today," I observed. Or "Your dad's recipes are so original. I'd love to know where he gets his ideas from."

That particular comment earned me a frown, but I was undeterred. Then I said aloud what I'd been thinking all afternoon. "I can't wait see the kitchen. It must be huge."

He snapped to attention. "You won't," he blurted, his tone as final as a slamming door.

"Won't what?" I felt so victorious that he'd deigned to speak to me that I barely even registered his scowl.

"You won't see the kitchen." He nodded toward the kitchen door, which loomed, shining, like the entrance to a priceless treasure trove. "Nobody is allowed in there except for me, Hughie, and Stella, Dad's other assistant baker. Dad keeps all his recipes under lock and key. Hughie and Stella never actually mix up the recipes; they just bake the premixed dough and help fill orders. And it took them *many* tries to pass Dad's baking test."

"So . . . it's true?" My voice betrayed my disbelief. "The Cookie Challenge is real?"

I couldn't help but say it with a hint of reverence. I'd heard rumors of the challenge Mr. Winston gave to wannabe assistant bakers—a baking test so difficult that a few unfortunate contenders had given up in tears. The way the challenge worked, supposedly, was that Mr. Winston picked out a bunch of ingredients at random, and the test taker had to use *only* those ingredients to make a delicious cookie.

Now it seemed that half the people in the store had their ears cocked, waiting to see if Flynn would share anything that might give a glimpse of Mr. Winston from "behind the curtain."

Flynn only shrugged nonchalantly. "Like I said. You'll never see the kitchen."

The anticipation that had fluttered inside me all day suddenly lost its wings. "But if I can't use the kitchen, how will I bake?"

"Don't ask me." Flynn heaved a sigh of frustration. He glanced at me, and for a millisecond, I thought a trace of regret flitted across his angular face. It was gone before I could blink. "This whole apprentice gig was Hughie's idea. Not mine. He said we needed the extra help. Talk to him if you're ready to quit."

"Wha . . . ?" I stiffened. "I'm *not* quitting. And as far as the baking goes, I'll find a way."

Flynn shook his head, as if my determination was as futile as waiting for a crumbled cookie to mend itself. "Don't get your hopes up."

We were staring at each other in a silent standoff when Hughie appeared at my side, cell phone in hand. I groaned inwardly, fearing he'd enlist me to take more pics for social media. Instead, he said, "We have an online delivery order for a dozen Sweet 'n' Salty cookies. From the Oyster Cove Museum."

"The museum?" I felt a rush of hope and wondered if Kalli

had anything to do with the order. I'd texted her a while ago with a grimacing face emoji in response to her *How's it going in Heaven?* text. This was just the sort of genius tactic she'd mastermind to get the scoop on my current state of mind.

"I'll deliver it," I said at the same moment Flynn said, "You can deliver it."

Hughie gave us an endearing smile and clasped his hands together. "Aw . . . it's so nice to see you two working well together."

I nearly laughed aloud. *Yeah, right.*

"Flynn, you'll help her get the delivery ready?" Hughie didn't wait for a reply before turning for the office.

I glanced at Flynn, who filled a delivery bag with cookies and slid it to me without even looking my way.

Fine, I thought. *The less he says at this point, the better.*

Once the warm bag was in my hands, I practically ran the two blocks to the museum. Inside the hushed space, Mrs. Torrence, the museum's curator, greeted me warmly and accepted the cookie order. I asked her if I could say hi to Kalli, and Mrs.

Torrence directed me to the back office. There, I found Kalli busy and beaming over the Samish basketry artifacts she was meticulously entering into an online inventory.

"This job is amazing," she gushed, but then saw my disgruntled expression. "Oh no. What's wrong?"

I sank into the chair across from her. "What's wrong is that I'm not doing *any* baking. Just social media stuff. And making deliveries, I guess." Kalli smiled, admitting that she had suggested the museum put through an order for cookies today. I thanked her for that, then told her all about Mr. Winston and Hughie—and Flynn, of course.

Kalli processed all of this wearing her classic worry brow, and squeezed my hand. "I'm sorry. I was afraid something like this would happen after your run-in with Flynn. It would've been better if you hadn't said anything."

"No way. I'll never regret speaking the truth." I waved my hand. "Enough about me. You're loving the museum so far?"

Kalli nodded, her face brightening as she told me how kind and helpful her colleagues were. I was happy at least one of us was having a good day. I wished I could stay and chat longer, but Kalli had more work to do and I needed to return to the shop.

I slogged back, wondering what sort of rude remark Flynn would make upon my return. Luckily, when I stepped into the store, Flynn was nowhere to be found and Mr. Winston's other assistant, Stella, was taking orders behind the counter.

"Mina!" Hughie said, coming out of the kitchen. "Thanks for making that delivery. You should head home now. I hope we didn't wear you out too much on your first day."

"Not at all," I responded, even though I was fighting back a yawn.

"Good." Hughie smiled at me. "We'll see you next Monday after school for more mentorship fun!"

I worried what sort of fun Hughie, Mr. Winston, and the shop's Instagram account might have in mind.

"Actually," I said, an idea forming, "I know the mentorship is supposed to be one day a week, but I'd like to come in tomorrow, if that's okay. And maybe I could come in other afternoons, too, if you need extra help?"

"Extra help," Hughie whispered in amazement, and clapped his hands. "You are a treasure. You come in as many days as you want. Just make sure it's all right with your parents and your school."

I nodded, shouldered my schoolbag, and stepped outside. Walking through town in the golden late-afternoon sunlight, I solidified my plan. As soon as I got home, I'd bake a batch of nankhatais. I'd bring them to the shop tomorrow afternoon and prove to Mr. Winston that I could handle any baking jobs he'd give me.

I passed Mrs. Yang's Korean BBQ, and a sign on the door made me stop in my tracks. The restaurant had been there for as long as I could remember, and Mrs. Yang liked to boast that she was as old as time itself. Her barbecue was delicious, and the restaurant was one of the most popular in Oyster Cove. So I felt a little sadness mingled with my excitement as I read the sign:

RETIRING AFTER FORTY YEARS. RESTAURANT SPACE

FOR SALE BY OWNER. INQUIRE WITHIN.

An available restaurant space. I couldn't wait to see the look on my father's face when I told him the news. This was just what we needed!

Then, as if Dad had known I was thinking about him, my cell buzzed with a text from him.

Where are you? When will you be home?

My stomach sank. Then I reminded myself that whatever disaster was happening at home, the restaurant news would make it all okay. With that thought in mind, I hurried down the sidewalk toward home.

Chapter Three

I heard the shrill wailing before I even opened our front door, and hesitated on the steps, tempted to linger outside. I remembered a time, not so long ago, when our house had been filled with enticing aromas instead of crying. A time when I couldn't wait for each afternoon, when I would put on my favorite KEEP CALM AND CURRY ON apron and cook dinner alongside Dad.

Now I caught a glimpse of Dad through the window. He stood in the kitchen with Amul and Banita strapped against his chest in the twin baby carrier, both of them squalling and red-faced. This man, who could dice an onion with epic speed and dexterity, was clumsily struggling to pour formula into bottles. His face was blotchy and perspiring, and the dismay and desperation in his eyes made me wonder if *he* was about to start bawling, too.

Feeling a stab of sympathy for him, I took a deep breath and opened the door.

"You're finally home!" Dad's relief was unmistakable, but so was his frustration. "What took you so long to get home from school? We're down to two diapers, and I have to run to the store . . ." His voice cratered into a sigh.

"Dad, didn't you remember?" I went to him and lifted Banita from the carrier, offering her the pacifier I'd grabbed from the kitchen table. She began sucking furiously, and I knew it would only be seconds before she spit it out to scream for the bottle. "I started my apprenticeship today after school." He shook his head blankly, so I added, "You signed the permission slip?"

Recognition dawned on his face. "Yes . . ." He nodded. "I forgot all about that. And . . . did you get the job you wanted, beti?"

"The baking job." I nodded. "Yes, but . . . well, the first day was a little complicated." Dad and I were close, and normally, I shared everything with him. But I didn't want to dwell on negatives right now. Not when he was already looking so stressed and I had a way to make it better. Instead, I gave him my cheeriest smile. "I have amazing news—"

"Good, good." He patted my cheek, his smile tired and distracted. Before I could tell him about Mrs. Yang's restaurant, or even about my plan to make nankhatais tonight, he was turning away to set Amul in his baby rocker, saying, "Could you feed them while I run to the store? Your mom should be home any minute."

"But—" One by one, the bubbles of excitement inside me were popping, bringing me back to reality. A year ago, my dad would've listened eagerly to how my day went as we cooked and baked together. He'd always defended my single-minded focus to Mom, who didn't approve of my shirking chores in favor of recipe inventing.

"She must listen when the muse speaks to her," he'd once told her after I'd gotten into trouble for baking when I'd been asked to clean my room.

Mom had clicked her tongue, warning Dad that he'd only spoil me by letting me give in to my "flights of fancy," as she called them. Dad had responded by chuckling and kissing her cheek.

"You married a man who has his own flights of fancy," he'd teased her. "And you've learned to put up with mine."

She'd laughed then, because it was true. Dad had once been an impulse chef himself, getting up in the middle of the night to cook when inspiration struck. But that was *before* the twins. Before my parents began to resemble zombies—walking and talking, but not all there. Seeing them like this was worrying, which was why, despite my urge to argue with him right now, I gave Dad a reluctant "Sure." The news about the restaurant *and* my nankhatais would have to wait.

As soon as Dad left, Banita spit out her binkie. Her face crinkled, her mouth opening in a silent, soon-to-be-deafening wail.

I set her in the rocker beside Amul and, with bottles in both my hands, fed them simultaneously. The babysitting safety course I'd taken back in sixth grade had helped prep me for the twins' feedings and diaper changes, but somehow, two babies seemed exponentially harder to handle than one. No sooner had I lifted Banita to my shoulder to burp her than Amul needed his diaper changed.

I've got this, I told myself, but the more the babies fussed, the more my conviction wavered. Just as my resolve was turning into mild panic, Mom walked through the door.

"Oh, my cuties!" After dropping a pile of lab reports onto the table, Mom first swept up Amul and then Banita, pressing her lips against their plump cheeks. "I've missed you so much!" She sank onto the couch in the family room, looking as tired as Dad.

"They just had their bottles." I sat down beside her, and she kissed my forehead.

"Thank goodness. I have hours of work to do tonight." She sighed. "I'm still trying to catch up."

Mom was a molecular biologist. She'd only returned to her job at MedVenire a few days ago, right after Nani, my grandma, had flown back to Delhi. Nani had been staying with us since the twins' birth and having her help had been a lifesaver. Which was why, now that she'd left, our house was even more chaotic than usual.

Dad's job as a freelance columnist for *Culinary Creations*, a gourmet cooking magazine, was flexible and part-time. He and Mom had decided that he'd stay home with the twins until they were old enough for day care. But looking at Mom's harried face, I was seriously doubting whether this had been a good idea for either one of them.

"How was your day today, beti?" she asked me now. But then she leaned her head back against the couch pillows, closing her eyes. "Just a ten-minute micronap, and . . ." Her voice faded, and a second later, her breathing deepened and slowed. The babies nestled against her chest, drifting off, too.

Taking advantage of the peace, I hurried into the kitchen to preheat the oven and set out the ingredients for my cookies. Feeling as if there was an hourglass draining my few minutes of free time away, I quickly measured out and poured flour and cardamom powder, powdered sugar, and a pinch of saffron into our stand mixer. After years of baking and cooking lessons from Dad, I moved seamlessly through the steps.

I chopped handfuls of pistachios and almonds, which I would sprinkle over the cookies before baking them. Then I melted some ghee, ready to pour the golden butter into the dry ingredients a little at a time until the dough moistened and thickened.

The instant I turned on the mixer, Banita startled into a wail. Amul followed with his own shrill cry, and Mom's eyes flew open.

"What—" She glanced toward the kitchen in dismay. "Mina, you woke the babies!"

I switched off the mixer, my cheeks heating with frustration. "I didn't mean to," I protested. "I only wanted to get some baking in while they napped."

Mom stood to rock the babies. "They're done napping now." She sighed. "And we have so many other more important things that need to be done around the house besides baking."

"Not more important to *me*," I blurted, then instantly regretted it when Mom frowned.

"And what about the other people in this house?" she asked. Her annoyed expression faded into exasperation. "I'm too tired for an argument. Finish up and then we can tackle the laundry together." She offered me a faint conciliatory smile, as if laundry would be a great mother-daughter bonding activity.

I nodded and then stared at the barely mixed dough in the bowl. I removed the beater from the mixer, resolving to mix the dough the rest of the way by hand. But my enthusiasm for the baking project had died. I finished prepping the cookies and slid them into the oven to bake just as Dad arrived home with the diapers.

"I picked up dinner, too," he said as he kissed Mom and set a rotisserie chicken on the counter.

I thought wistfully of the fantastic dinners of tikka masala and palak paneer Dad and I had made together in the months leading up to the twins' birth. It felt like forever since we'd had home-cooked anything. I swallowed my disappointment, knowing that saying anything out loud would only earn me another disapproving look from Mom. Instead, I helped Dad plate the chicken alongside some ninety-second instant rice with veggies. We ate quickly, taking turns holding the babies, but talk was made impossible by the twins' fussiness.

When the timer for the oven buzzed, I leapt up to take out my cookies. Despite my frantic baking prep, they'd turned out perfectly.

"When did you find time to bake cookies, beti?" Dad asked in surprise.

Before I could answer, Mom shook her head. "When the babies were *supposed* to be napping."

Dad gave me a stern look, but I could tell the attempt at scolding wasn't real, especially when he snatched a cookie from the tray.

"Svaadisht." Dad smiled approvingly. "Delicious."

They weren't the prettiest cookies I'd ever baked, but Dad was right. When I tasted them, they were as delicious as they'd always been. Mom, though, didn't look impressed. She was too busy trying to console a crying Amul.

"We've got to get them down for the night," she said to Dad, who nodded. Dad made for the stairs with Banita in his arms but glanced back at the kitchen (and the cookies) longingly.

"Do the dishes, please, Mina," Mom said as she followed him with Amul. "And start another load of laundry."

"But—"

One look from her, and I bit back a protest. Sighing, I grabbed a Tupperware container to store my cookies for tomorrow. My gaze landed on the tattered recipe book sitting on the kitchen counter. I picked it up, my heart panging at the light layer of dust on the cover. *Mina and Dad's Recipes* was scrawled in messy, childish writing across the cover—*my* handwriting from way back in second grade. I opened the book to the very first recipe for apple halwa, which was an applesauce-like dessert with ghee and sugar. Dad had started off teaching me the easiest recipes, and through the years and pages of the book, the recipes grew more challenging.

As I flipped through the butter-and-batter-smudged pages, a restlessness surged through me, an itch I needed to scratch.

How long had it been since Dad and I had added a recipe to our book? The last entry had been days before the twins' births. Sometimes, it felt like there was a measuring cup inside me that only the act of baking filled. When the measuring cup was empty, *I* felt emptier, too. I brushed my hand across the crinkled pages, then slapped the book's cover shut.

"I miss cooking with you, too, beti." Dad's voice was quiet, and I turned to discover him standing behind me, a wistful expression on his face. He gestured toward the recipe book.

I smiled, feeling a renewed sense of determination. This was my chance to share the news I'd been holding in for hours. "Speaking of cooking," I began, my pulse surging. "I saw a sign at Mrs. Yang's Korean BBQ today. She's putting the space up for sale."

"Really?" Dad shook his head with disappointment. "What a shame. She will be sorely missed, and so will her delicious food."

"I know," I said quickly. "But, Dad, the restaurant space is for *sale*." I emphasized the last part, thinking that maybe he was simply too dazed from lack of sleep to comprehend what that meant. "It's a great location downtown, with a steady flow of foot traffic." I waited for his face to light up with realization, but when it didn't, I prodded, "Perfect for our restaurant?"

"Ah." He nodded slowly, rubbing his eyes. "Yes. Our restaurant. I thought we'd have it by now."

"With me helping plan the menus," I reminded Dad. I knew my father had been dreaming of the new restaurant ever since he and Mom moved to America, before I'd even been born. He'd sold his restaurant back in India but had been determined to open a new one here in Oyster Cove. He'd envisioned an Indian fusion restaurant that combined all the best spices and dishes of India blended with other cuisines. Dad had told me last year that we had savings enough to open the new restaurant and had started looking for the right location. But then—surprise!—the twins had come along.

"Now we *can* have the restaurant. You should call Mrs. Yang. ASAP." My voice held a firm certainty and hopefulness.

"Mmmm." Dad offered me a slow, thoughtful smile. Not at all the gushing display of enthusiasm I'd been expecting.

"It'll be amazing!" I continued just as the baby monitor on the counter crackled to life with a baby's cry.

"I'll be right there!" Dad called, hurrying back upstairs.

I watched him go, mulling over his strange reaction. I'd expected him to be on the phone already, dialing Mrs. Yang. Now was our time for action, and he'd just left the room. It seemed unfathomable, but then again, so did the fact that we'd had twins. When would our lives get back to normal? And how could I make sure they did?

I flopped onto my bed and stared up at the ceiling as Kalli's jubilant voice came through the phone.

"You wouldn't believe some of the artifacts I got to see today," she was saying. "There was a potlatch bowl and these amazing painted masks and rattles . . . I got so lucky with this job."

"I'm so glad, Kalli. It sounds awesome." While I felt a genuine happiness for her, my voice was strained. Of course, Kalli picked up on it immediately.

"Hey, I'm sure your job will end up being just as cool, too."

Her tone downshifted into sympathy. "You had a rough first day, but it'll get better."

My laugh was tinged with doubt. "It'll only get better when Flynn quits giving me the evil eye."

"I don't get what his deal is," Kalli said. There was a pause, and I imagined Kalli tapping the tip of her nose, something she often did when she was worrying. "You don't think you offended him somehow?"

"He's the one who offended *me*!"

"Right" came her quick response. "It's just . . . sometimes you can be . . ."

"What?" I prodded. "A know-it-all?"

"I was going to say assertive," Kalli offered tactfully. She knew me better than anyone, and I loved her for her ability to appreciate every aspect of my personality, even traits others might consider shortcomings.

I laughed. "No, I was *not* too assertive with him. Anyway, I don't believe a person can be *too* assertive. Seriously, how will I ever accomplish what I want to in life if I let other people hold the reins?" Now it was Kalli's turn to laugh. Then I whooped as I was struck with sudden inspiration. "I know how to fix this! I can't believe I didn't think of this before." I grinned. "I can Jedi mind trick him with my taste buds!"

"Um . . . what?" Kalli asked. "Oh . . . you mean that cool thing you do where you figure out every single ingredient that's in food just by taste alone?"

"You got it."

It was a "talent" I'd inherited from Dad—something he'd challenge me with whenever he tried a brand-new recipe. I could taste a dish—pretty much any dish—without knowing what had gone into it, and I could name its ingredients.

"Mina, I love it when you use the Foodie Force." Kalli's tone was gentle, and I could tell she was building up to a "but." I could always count on Kalli to offer the flip side of every positive coin. "But I'm not sure it can change anything with Flynn."

"Of course it can! It will impress him, and then I can get this whole situation under control. Turn things around. In fact, I already baked a batch of nankhatais to bring to the shop tomorrow."

"Ooh, good plan," Kalli said encouragingly. "Flex your cookie muscles for them. But maybe you should try to connect with Flynn before that. Like at school, without the shop's hecticness?"

"Great idea." I smiled. "He does seem way more stressed when he's at the shop."

By the time I hung up, I felt better. No matter how abrasive Flynn was tomorrow, I'd never give in to annoyance. I'd counter every one of his frowns with a smile and kill him with kindness, one nankhatai at a time.

Chapter Four

Tuesday morning at school passed in a blur as I waited for my chance to talk to Flynn. I'd nearly forgotten my cookies in the chaos at home. My parents had slept through their alarm, and we'd all had to scramble to get ready amid the twins' protests about their overdue morning feedings. Still, I'd managed to swipe the Tupperware container of cookies from the kitchen counter just as I rushed out the door.

Now that the lunch period had finally arrived, I hurriedly ate my sandwich as I waited for Flynn, Trent, and Will to head for the archery range, like they did almost every day during lunch.

Flynn wasn't on the archery team with Trent and Will, but I knew he liked to hang out at the range with them, watching them shoot. As soon as Flynn stood to toss his trash, I stood, too, my pulse quickening.

"May the Foodie Force be with you." Kalli gave me a thumbs-up while Fabiana and Jane offered me encouraging smiles.

I thanked my friends and, Tupperware in hand, walked out of the cafeteria. The indoor archery range was in a long, narrow room abutting the gym. As I reached its doorway, I reminded myself to stand tall. Today was a new day, and I was going to give Flynn the benefit of the doubt.

I rounded the corner with a cheery "Hey, Flynn!" My voice echoed off the range's empty walls with surprising force. Trent, whose back was to me, startled and shot his arrow wildly, missing the target at the other end of the room by a good six feet.

Trent lowered his recurve bow and turned to face me with a joking "Thanks, Mina."

"Looks like you could use more practice anyway," I quipped playfully in response, to which he and Will laughed.

Flynn, though, who was sitting in a folding chair by the door, stayed stone-faced, his eyes two storm-tossed seas.

"Do you ever shoot?" I asked him in an attempt to make friendly conversation. I watched as Will let an arrow fly that landed just outside the red bull's-eye.

"No." There was a bitterness to his tone that surprised me.

"Why not? It looks fun to me." This only made his expression stormier, and I caught Trent and Will exchanging an "uh-oh" glance. Feeling like I was rapidly losing ground, I held out the Tupperware container toward Flynn. "I brought you some cookies. Homemade."

"Cookies!" Trent blurted. "I *love* cookies!" He started toward me but stopped when he caught sight of Flynn's flatlining mouth. "Right . . ." he mumbled, then motioned to Will. "We're gonna go grab some more paper targets. Be back in a minute."

The two of them tiptoed past Flynn and me to the door, with Trent offering me a small smile of sympathy as they left.

Flynn didn't make a move to take the cookies. Instead, he pulled an arrow from one of the tubelike arrow holsters, rolling it between his fingers. He stared down at it, and a flicker of frustration tightened his brow. Understanding dawned on me. He *wanted* to shoot. That much was clear.

"Why don't you?" I said, motioning to the target. "Go ahead. Try it."

For a second, he looked startled, and I knew I'd hit the nail on the head. Then he frowned, muttering a barely audible "Why bother?" He stood up with a grumbled "I have to go."

"Wait! You forgot the cookies!" He stopped and glanced back at me. "Listen," I went on, trying to be brave. "We got off on the wrong foot. But since we're going to be working together at the shop, I—"

"I don't want to talk about the shop," he interrupted, his tone final. He turned to go again.

Frustration burbled inside me. "Would you hold on a second?" I reached out a hand to stop him. I brushed his shoulder, and a sudden electric heat flashed through me. I pulled back, scolding myself. I could *not* let his cuteness get in the way of my mission. "This is a peace offering. You don't like me, for whatever stupid reason. But at least try one." Before he could protest, I practically shoved the cookie container toward him.

With a look of resignation, Flynn popped the lid on the container and peered inside. Confusion, and a hint of amusement, swept across his face. "Well . . . I've never seen cookies like these before." I bristled, but before I could respond, he added, "But they're definitely *not* edible."

"Wh—" My words died as Flynn tilted the open container toward me. I stared inside and, instead of my beautiful cookies, saw . . .

"Baby bottles!" I cringed. My parents always kept extra sterilized bottles in a container on the counter, ready for use. *"No!"* I groaned. "I must've taken the wrong container." I tried to recall if I'd seen one or two containers on the counter this morning, but my memories were a rushed, hazy blur.

Flynn's lips twitched like he was tempted to smile, but he didn't give in to it. Instead, he handed the container back to me. "It doesn't matter." He shrugged. "I'm sure the cookies you made were fine for your family. They'll enjoy them."

I stared at him, my embarrassment swiftly replaced with broiling anger. "What's that supposed to mean?" I snapped. "That *my* cookies aren't good enough for *your* shop?"

He paused. "It's not something you can understand." His voice was quiet and colored with regret.

"How would you know?" My spine became a ruler as I stared him down. "You've been nothing but rude to me, when you know *nothing* about me. I'm sure this has completely escaped your attention, because it's obvious now that you're completely stuck on yourself, but I was actually looking forward to working with you." His mouth fell open, and I took a little satisfaction in seeing him rendered momentarily speechless. "I thought it would be fun. I was giving you the benefit of the doubt." I turned for the door. "But you don't deserve it."

I marched out the door without a second glance. Gone was my determination to extend an olive branch to Flynn Winston. Gone was my resolve to kill him with kindness. If he wanted to wage a battle against me, I'd bring my baking battalions and then some. This meant war.

*   *   *

That afternoon, I didn't linger outside the shop to savor the irresistible scent of baking cookies. Instead, I walked through A Batch Made in Heaven's door with steely determination. My heart whirred faster than a high-speed mixer when I felt Flynn's eyes following me as I marched past the counter. But I refused to look in his direction, instead focusing on Mr. Winston and Hughie.

Mr. Winston was at the back of the shop with Hughie, posing for photos. There was a movable scenic backdrop behind him, of an impressive stainless-steel kitchen. There was a cherry-red KitchenAid mixer on the foldout table before him, and he was holding a spatula in one hand and a bowl of eggs in the other.

"Perfect timing, Mina!" Hughie wasted no time handing me his phone. "I've got to finish today's post ASAP."

I nodded, holding back a sigh. Hopefully, now that I knew the routine, today's pics would go quickly. Mr. Winston was already getting into position for a photo as I asked, "Mr. Winston, wouldn't it be more interesting to take these photos while you're inventing recipes for real?"

Mr. Winston huffed at that. "Followers want pictures that take them *out* of reality. Not ones that remind them of it." But— was it just me, or was his neck turning bright red under his chef's collar?

Hughie glanced at Mr. Winston, cleared his throat, and said offhandedly, "Oh, all influencer photos on social media are staged these days."

Not wanting to argue with either one of them, I snapped the obligatory pics, added filters, and posted them to the shop's feed.

"Great!" Hughie said approvingly while Mr. Winston gave a cursory nod before disappearing into the Cookie Vault. "Now we can start on tomorrow's blog post—"

"Hughie," Flynn interrupted, appearing at his side. "Sorry, but we're busy and I, um . . ." He paused, glancing at me with a discomfort he didn't even try to hide. I stiffened. "Dad needs my help in the kitchen while he finishes working on his newest recipe. Remember?"

He gave Hughie a pointed look, and I wondered just how desperately he was trying to avoid me.

"Oh. The newest recipe." Understanding dawned on Hughie's face. "For the Cookie of the Day. Right. Mina and I will handle the sales. You go help your dad."

I looked back and forth between the two of them, getting the distinct impression that they were speaking in code. Maybe this *was* just Flynn's plot to avoid me, but there was an undercurrent to this whole situation that suddenly seemed like much more than that. Something weird was going on, but I couldn't put my finger on what.

Flynn promptly disappeared into the Cookie Vault. Then Hughie and I tackled the growing line of customers while Stella made sure the dining room tables stayed clean. At least with Hughie working the cash register and taking orders, I had the chance to be more "hands-on," carefully taking warm cookies from the glass display case and plating them for customers. When Flynn reappeared at the counter, he looked even more frustrated than before (if that was possible).

"It's your turn to talk to him," Flynn told Hughie.

Hughie let out a low whistle. "Trouble with your—" He froze, then stumbled over his next words. "Your dad's new recipe?"

Flynn frowned. "It's finished. It's just never good enough," he mumbled.

Hughie smiled at Flynn. "Oh, now, I doubt that." Then he glanced toward the Cookie Vault. "Here comes your dad."

Mr. Winston appeared with a platter of luscious-looking cookies, and Hughie clanged an enormous cowbell hanging above the back counter. "Attention! Attention!" Hughie called out. "It's time to unveil the Cookie of the Day."

A hush fell over the customers as they waited for Mr. Winston to name the cookie, as he did for every new recipe.

Mr. Winston opened his mouth, then shut it again. He glanced at Flynn and leaned toward him to whisper, "What's this one called?"

How strange, I thought. Mr. Winston had forgotten the name of his brand-new recipe?

"You're Mocha My Dreams Come True," Flynn whispered back to Mr. Winston.

Mr. Winston nodded and then announced the name, to the

great applause of everyone in the shop. At the sight of the mocha cookies, customers offered up a collective "ooooh" of delight. The cookies were tantalizing in their dark chocolatey-ness, shaped like mini muffins, and seemed to have warm ganache oozing from their middles. Their rich, cocoa aroma filled the shop, making my mouth water.

"I want one of those!" Half a dozen people were already calling dibs on the cookies, and surprisingly, this brought a rare smile to Flynn's face.

"There's another batch coming in a few," Flynn said to stave off cookie panic while Mr. Winston nodded.

I plated the first of the cookies, which looked even more irresistible up close. I hesitated before handing it to an eager customer, and as I did, I caught Flynn looking at me, a glimmer of amusement in his eyes.

"You want to try one." It was a statement rather than a question.

I paused, not wanting to concede that he was right, but the cookies looked *so* tempting—mini chocolate volcanoes overflowing with heavenly cocoa lava. And the moment I'd been waiting for had finally arrived. This was the perfect chance to impress Flynn with my ingredient-tasting talent.

"Just one," I said noncommittally, even though my taste buds already tingled in anticipation. I plucked a cookie from the platter and bit into a rich chocolate layer to the pudding-like, creamy center. Closing my eyes, I chewed slowly, absorbing every nuance of flavor.

When I opened my eyes again, I'd solved the ingredient puzzle, and it was time to prove it to Flynn. "Finely ground espresso," I began. "Dark chocolate morsels and semisweet, too. A splash of hazelnut extract." Flynn's eyes widened. A smile spread across my face. "Heavy cream, eggs, baking powder, brown sugar, Dutch-processed cocoa powder, flour, vanilla, and the tiniest pinch of cinnamon."

Flynn blinked in surprise. Then he seemed to give himself a mental shake. "Impressive. But you missed one." His cool tone didn't sound that impressed, though, which made what I was about to do all the sweeter.

"Oh, right!" I folded my arms and grinned. "You mean the toffee bits!"

For several seconds, Flynn's lips moved without making any sound. Then, after a quick glance at Mr. Winston, Flynn motioned me away from the sales counter. Mr. Winston took over the register, his eyes following Flynn and me (a little nervously, I thought) as Flynn led me to the back of the shop.

"Okay," Flynn whispered when we were safely beyond earshot of the other customers. "Where'd you get my—my dad's recipe? He just invented it today."

"I didn't." It was satisfying to see Flynn so discombobulated. "I have a knack for guessing ingredients." At his skeptical expression, I added, "I tried to tell you before. Baking is my thing." I stuck my hands on my hips and stared him down. "What? Is it so hard to believe that somebody could guess your dad's secret ingredients?" I nodded toward the menu behind the sales counter. "I know he doesn't list all the ingredients on the menu, either. There's pumpkin and a pinch of chai in the Falling for You snickerdoodles, and cornflakes in the Cookie Monster, and—"

"Stop!" Flynn hissed, glancing over my shoulder to make sure no one else was privy to our conversation. "No one knows the secret ingredients." He shook his head in disbelief. "No one."

"Except me." I looked right at him, daring him to deny it.

He broke my gaze. "You—you haven't told anybody else about this, have you?"

"Why—" I started, then suddenly realized what he was implying. "Oh . . . I get it. You think I'm going to spill your dad's secret recipes to the world. Is that it?" When he didn't respond, I shook my head. "Wow . . . I didn't think it was possible for you to insult me any more than you already have, but—"

"Whoa." Flynn held up his hands. "I wasn't trying to insult you. I just . . . Look. I'm sorry. I'm sure I'm coming across as a total jerk. I snapped at you at the archery range earlier, and now . . ." He ran a hand through his hair, his expression softening. "I can see how this all looks, and I wish I could explain everything, but—" He shook his head. "It's . . . not you."

"Then start giving me the benefit of the doubt." Our eyes

locked, and I felt heat rushing to my cheeks. The dusky pools of his eyes threatened to hypnotize me.

The sound of Kalli calling my name broke our face-off. Flynn blinked and turned toward the sales counter. I noticed a redness about his ears as he walked away.

"Mina, you're not going to believe this!" Kalli was usually so soft-spoken, but now her voice echoed loudly through the shop. "I ran all the way from home. Look what I just found online!" She thrust her cell phone up to my face.

"'Join Cookie Crumbles's quest for its next great cookie,'" I read aloud from the screen.

Cookie Crumbles was one of the best-known cookie brands in the country. Their cookies graced the shelves of every grocery store, and there was always a box of Cookie Crumbles Choco-Crisps in our pantry. Despite his refined tastes, the Crisps were Dad's favorite midnight snack.

"A cookie baking contest?" I asked Kalli.

She nodded so hard that her straight black hair flew in all directions. "Isn't it perfect for you?" She read aloud: "'Entrants submit a cookie recipe first, and finalists are chosen to make a trip to Seattle to participate in a live cookie bake-off. It'll be streamed on Cookie Crumbles's YouTube channel. And . . .'" She bounced on her toes. "'The winner gets a thousand-dollar shopping spree at Seattle's Baking and Culinary Arts Depot.'"

"Wow." My heart slammed against my ribs. The first thing that popped into my head was: *I can win this contest.* The second was: *Dad's restaurant.* I beamed at Kalli. "Can you imagine all the supplies I could buy with the prize money? I could give them to Dad, for our restaurant."

Kalli paused. "Wait. Your family's opening the restaurant? I thought that wasn't happening anymore."

"It hasn't happened *yet*, only because it's been so chaotic since the twins came. But now Mrs. Yang's restaurant is up for sale. It's the perfect location, and as soon as Dad calls her, everything will fall into place. The prize money will be the icing on the cake."

"Mina." Kalli's tone was cautious. "It might not be as easy as that—"

"Sure it would!" My pulse drummed happily as my mind filled with visions of me working alongside Dad in our restaurant. He'd be making his famous rogan josh while I prepared beautiful plates of dessert for our waiting customers. We'd laugh together, and Dad—the lively, fun Dad I'd known before the twins were born—would be back. "It will be perfect."

Kalli didn't seem so sure. "You always say that, but"—she sighed—"then you end up disappointed when things don't work the way you imagined. Remember your history project last year? You got so upset that your papier-mâché Taj Mahal didn't look *exactly* like the real deal. You smashed the whole thing before anyone else even saw it!"

"That was different." I stiffened. "I had a vision of what I wanted it to be, and . . ." My voice faded as Kalli gently squeezed my hand.

"Maybe this time try not to expect too much?" she offered. "Just see what happens when you tell your parents about the contest?"

I slid my hand from hers, a nettle of irritation pricking me.

Did Kalli always have to be a killjoy? Couldn't she share in my excitement just once without the doubts?

"I'm not going to tell them," I blurted, deciding on the spot. "I'll keep it a secret so that when I win, it'll be an even bigger surprise." Kalli's brow creased with concern, but I peered at her phone screen, searching for more details. "So when are the recipe entries due?"

Kalli faltered. "That's the thing. I only saw the contest online today, but it's been going on for a while already. Recipes have to be emailed to Cookie Crumbles by next Friday, October fifteenth."

"Next Friday?" I practically shrieked, causing Flynn to glance up sharply from the cash register. I sucked in a breath, doing a mental tally, then straightened with resolve. "Okay. That's one out-of-this-world recipe in ten days. Totally doable!"

"How?" Kalli countered. "It's a miracle if you get five minutes to yourself at home. You said that you can't concentrate with the twins crying all the time."

I thought about this, then grinned. "Easy fix. Mr. Winston's

Cookie Challenge." I nodded decisively. "I have to take it. That way I can bake in the Cookie Vault!"

A split second's uncertainty skittered across Kalli's face, but she smiled. "If anyone can do it, you can."

"Thanks, Kalli," I said, giving her a quick hug. I offered to snag her a free You're Mocha My Dreams Come True cookie, but Kalli waved me off and bought one herself.

After Kalli had left, I took a deep breath and marched over to Mr. Winston, ready to execute my plan.

"Mr. Winston." My tone was firm and decisive, and he paused in his plating of cookies to look at me. "I'd like to take your Cookie Challenge."

My announcement was met with dumbfounded silence as everyone within earshot paused to stare at me. As far as I knew, no one had taken the challenge since Hughie and Stella had passed it.

Mr. Winston's eyes widened. "I—I see," he began, then cleared his throat awkwardly. "Well then . . ." He glanced quickly at Flynn, who I'd noticed had turned two shades paler than usual.

My eyes flitted from Flynn to Mr. Winston in confusion. What was going on? Why were both of them behaving so oddly?

"Fine." Flynn's voice was clipped, with an unexpectedly hard edge. "Your house. Your oven. Your ingredients. Five p.m. this evening."

"But . . . but . . ." *I might not be able to bake at home*, I wanted to say.

Before I could stammer out the rest of the words, Flynn said, "Take it or leave it."

I saw then that he was immovable. If I gave excuses now, I'd never have this chance again.

I set my jaw and met his eyes, unflinching. "I'll take it."

He nodded, then exchanged a brief glance with his dad. Clearly, neither one of them was happy with this new development, but I wasn't about to let that intimidate me. Flynn turned back to me. "You should go home. Get ready."

I nodded, relieved. I needed to make sure I had enough ingredients on hand. Plus—I cringed as I thought of the disastrous mess of diapers, bottles, and baby toys that littered our kitchen and family room—a little cleanup wouldn't hurt, either.

I hurriedly grabbed my schoolbag and coat. But I paused at the shop's doorway, watching Flynn and Mr. Winston as they spoke in low voices behind the sales counter. Mr. Winston's face looked uncharacteristically worried while Flynn's was simply exasperated. Something strange was going on at A Batch Made in Heaven, and I had the distinct impression that my Cookie Challenge had just made it worse.

Chapter Five

"How could we be out of cocoa powder?" I cried, staring into our near-empty pantry with mounting panic.

Dad paced the family room with crying Banita, patting her back. "I'm sorry, beti." His voice was gravelly with tiredness. "It's been a while since I've gone food shopping."

"Mr. Winston is going to be here any second!" I glanced at my phone, willing the 4:59 on the screen to stay put. "I was hoping I'd have enough good ingredients for him to choose from."

We were out of cardamom, too. I'd forgotten that I'd used the last of it for my nankhatais yesterday. And my dad had stress-eaten all the cookies today, so I couldn't even present *them* as ingredients. I pressed my forehead against the pantry door. What was I going to do?

Then the doorbell rang. I was out of time.

I groaned as I walked to the front door, opened it—and found Flynn standing on our porch.

"Oh!" I exclaimed, my face heating. "I thought—" I swallowed. This was *not* a good sign. "Where's your dad?"

"Couldn't make it." Flynn's tone was matter-of-fact as he stepped inside.

"But . . . isn't he the only one who gives the Cookie Challenge?" I asked.

Flynn's glower was instant. "Look, do you want to do this or not?"

"Yes!" I blurted, even as I thought, *This is going to be a disaster.* "Come into the kitchen."

He followed me through the family room and into the kitchen, where Dad was struggling to buckle Banita into her rocker while Amul fussed in his.

Dad absently welcomed Flynn, then turned to me. "I'll run out to get some groceries if you can mind the babies for a few minutes?"

My heart sank. I was sure Flynn wouldn't want to be bothered by two fretting babies. "I—"

"Sure thing, Mr. Kapur," Flynn said before I could finish. "We can handle it." Then—shocker—he bent over Banita's rocker to offer her a smile. Banita gave him a gummy, drooly grin back.

I forced my mouth not to fall open in surprise. Dad looked relieved, and he left with the briefest wave.

"He seemed like he could use a break," Flynn said as we heard the car pulling out of our driveway.

I nodded. "There's crying all the time," I conceded. "From the babies, I mean. Not my dad." I cringed inwardly.

Flynn laughed. "It must be hard with two of them." Still, there was a longing in his voice. "I'm an only child, and I always wanted a little brother or sister. Babies are so wise, you know? My theory is that they've got it all figured out. Like, how brilliant is it that they've masterminded how to be fed, rocked, and pretty much entertained by us all day long?"

"Baby geniuses?" I asked skeptically. But I couldn't help staring as he gently dangled a rattle in front of the mesmerized Banita. Flynn's eyes were lit with the same impish cheeriness I recognized from when he was around his friends at school. The transformation brightened his face. This Flynn was so different from the glowering Flynn I'd been butting heads with at the shop. My breath faltered as he made a goofy face at Banita and she cooed in response. I laughed in spite of myself.

"She likes you," I said, surprised.

His laugh was short. "That makes one of you, at least."

My cheeks flamed. "I don't *dislike* you." I couldn't meet his eyes, and his body tensed.

"But I killed my role model vibe with you, didn't I?"

I shrugged. "I'm pretty confident the rest of the student body still thinks you hung the moon." He scoffed, shaking his head, until I added, "It's the cookies."

He snorted. "Cookie bias?"

"Totally. No one can think clearly around freshly baked cookies."

He laughed but then grew serious. "So without the cookies, you're saying nobody would like me?"

"Oh. No. That's not what I meant," I backpedaled, feeling a pang of guilt.

"It doesn't matter," he said gruffly. I sensed that I'd upset him again. "So . . ." He focused on me. "Let's get started. Can you show me what's in your pantry?"

"Oh!" My stomach clenched. "Can we at least wait for my dad to get back? He's gonna pick up some cocoa powder."

A flicker of sympathy crossed Flynn's face, and I thought he might relent and say we could wait. But then the flicker vanished, replaced by steely indifference. "You can make something without cocoa powder. A good baker should always be able to improvise a recipe at the last minute."

How do you know? I wanted to ask. His dad invented all the recipes, so what expertise could Flynn possibly have? Instead, I clamped my mouth shut and gestured to the pantry so Flynn could start choosing ingredients.

Flynn reached past me into the pantry, brushing my arm, and a jolt of electricity shot through me. I caught the scent of cinnamon and sugar in his hair. I leaned against the door frame to steady myself as he pulled a bag of macadamia nuts from a shelf.

Get a grip, I told myself.

Flynn selected flour, sugar, eggs, baking powder—the basics. Whew. Then he added a container of oatmeal, the nuts, and tossed me an orange from our fruit bowl on the counter. "What could you do with these?" he asked.

I stared down at the orange, waiting for ideas to flow, easy as waterfalls, the way they did whenever I felt the zing of baking inspiration. Instead, I felt only the roaring rapids of panic, unfamiliar and strange. This *never* happened to me. This kitchen had always been the place in our house that I felt *most* at home. Only lately, everything in our house had felt off, including me. "Um . . ." I sucked in a breath. *Don't blow it*, I thought. "Um . . ."

"Come on," Flynn said impatiently. "You have to come up with ideas quicker than that." A few more seconds passed as I floundered, and then he huffed impatiently. "You can't do it."

"Yes I *can*! If you'd give me a *minute*!" I held the orange in a death grip now, resisting the urge to launch it directly at Flynn's smug face. "You know what? Forget it. You were never going to give me a fair shot, anyway."

"Hey, it's not my fault you're unprepared," he said offhandedly.

That was it. The last straw. "You . . . *you* . . . This *is* your fault!" I stared furiously at him, my heart racing. "You've been a jerk to me from the start. How am I supposed to think straight with you relishing every wrong move I make?"

Amul, who'd been napping, woke with a wail. I marched over to lift him from the Pack 'n Play, and turned back to Flynn. "You came here tonight to make sure I'd fail the Cookie Challenge." My eyes locked on his as I waited to see if he'd admit it. "Didn't you?"

His eyebrows shot up, and although he was frowning, there was a startled regret in his expression. "I . . . I . . ." He dropped his gaze to the floor. "It's complicated."

"You *were* going to fail me. I knew it," I mumbled. "I'm never setting foot in your shop again. I'll ask Mr. Imari for a different mentorship. I wish I'd never gotten the job at your shop in the first place."

"Me too!" he blurted. But his tone was more hurt than angry, which confused me all the more. As he turned for the door, he mumbled what sounded like "You don't understand." Then he added as clear as day, "I'll tell my dad and Hughie you won't be coming back to the shop." He hung his head as he stepped over the threshold, adding a quiet "Trust me. It won't surprise them at all."

Disappointingly, the door clicked shut before he could hear my sulky "Fine."

As Amul fussed in my arms, I leaned against the counter, fuming. A second later, Dad walked in with grocery bags, already holding the cocoa powder out to me. I didn't take it. One look at my face and he knew something was wrong. "What happened?" he asked, setting down his bags to sweep Amul into his arms. "What is it, beti?"

It was on the tip of my tongue to tell him about the whole fight with Flynn, but how could I? Dumping my problems on him wasn't going to fix anything. It would only make him and

Mom more stressed, and I couldn't do that to them. I had to be strong enough for all of us right now.

"Nothing," I muttered as I turned to leave the kitchen. But I couldn't help adding, "Why couldn't we have just had the stupid cocoa powder?"

I woke the next morning to the soft pattering of a steady autumn rainfall. Last night's baking fiasco came back to me with sickening force. I sat up groggily and checked my phone. It was 5:00 a.m., and I felt like I'd barely slept at all.

I stared out the window at the rain gliding down the pane. My bay window offered a partial view of the Sound. Mist shrouded the pines and Pacific madrone trees that graced the shoreline. There was nothing better than baking a batch of comfort cookies on a dreary gray day like this. With a grunt of resentment, I wondered what sort of cookies Mr. Winston was baking at A Batch Made in Heaven. He was probably at the shop now, filling the Cookie Vault with the wonderful scent of melting butter and sugar.

Suddenly, adrenaline surged through my veins. Mr. Winston probably *was* at the shop right now. And Flynn probably wasn't.

I threw on my clothes, brushed my hair, and haphazardly splashed water on my face. I raced down the stairs, and when I rounded the corner to the family room, I saw Mom nestled on the couch, both babies drowsing in her lap.

"Sorry if I was loud," I whispered.

She gave me an exhausted smile. "No matter. They got up for their morning feeding an hour ago." She took in my clothes and the schoolbag flung over my shoulder. "Where are you off to at this hour?"

"A Batch Made in Heaven," I said hurriedly, already scrambling for the door.

"Don't tell me they have you working *before* school." Her tone was instantly disapproving. "Do I need to talk to Mr. Winston?"

"No, no, Mom." I hadn't exactly mentioned to my parents that the mentorship was only once a week. They couldn't make me come home to do chores if I was at a school-sponsored mentorship. The fewer details I told them, the better. Now I bent to give

Mom a quick kiss on the cheek. "This is all my idea. It's an extra project I'm working on at the shop. For the mentorship."

She nodded, sinking back against the cushions. "That's good, beti . . ." She was already drifting off to sleep again.

I shut the door, relieved that Mom had been too tired to ask more questions. Then I felt a stab of guilt at my deception. But I wouldn't think about that now. I had a plan, and I was going to make it work this time.

The rain slowly eased, the clouds lifted, and the sunrise cast rose-gold light across the Sound as I walked to the shop. I took comfort and courage from the cheerful glow and distant sound of lapping water. Several people were sitting on benches, sipping coffee and chatting before work. There were other people on boat decks in the harbor, preparing for a morning sail, eager to take advantage of the improving weather. I caught sight of our own little skiff bobbing in the water and raised my hand in a silent greeting. *We'll take you for a ride soon*, I thought, but in reality I had no idea when Dad would have the time. I turned away, quashing my urge to walk down to the dock and unmoor our boat right now. It would have to wait. Right now, I had work to do at the shop. Without Flynn around to throw me off balance, I'd be able to prove to Mr. Winston what a good baker I was, once and for all.

The shop had just opened for the day, but there were no customers yet. I stepped inside the empty dining room. Any minute, it would be bustling with early risers seeking out an ooey-gooey treat to start their morning.

"Hello?" I called out. "Mr. Winston?"

No one answered, but then the door to the Cookie Vault caught my eye. I couldn't believe it. The door was open a crack, and music was wafting from inside, along with the irresistible scent of freshly baked cookies.

"Mr. Winston?" I knocked on the Cookie Vault's door but got no answer. Slowly, I peeked around the door. "Flynn!" I blurted in surprise. He was standing at the Vault's enormous stainless-steel island, scooping mounds of chocolate chip cookie dough onto baking sheets.

Flynn's head shot up from his work. At the sight of me in the doorway, his eyes widened.

"I was looking for your dad." I took in the scene before me: ingredients scattered across the counter, an open notebook filled with scribbled measurements and baking notes. "Is that your dad's recipe book? What are you doing with it?" I took a step closer and studied the notebook, suddenly recognizing Flynn's handwriting. I'd seen him jot down notes at the shop when people called in delivery orders. "Wait . . ." My pulse jolted. "Those are *your* recipes!"

"Shhhh." He rushed out the kitchen door, hurried to the shop's window, and flipped the sign from OPEN to CLOSED. He was back in an instant and ushered me into the Vault, closing the door behind us. He glanced at the trays of dough, probably wondering if he could get away with any other explanation besides the obvious one. He sighed. "I guess this means the secret is out." He collapsed onto a stool and ran a hand through his hair, which immediately streaked it with flour.

I stared at him, my mind tumbling as fast as a whisk beating

eggs. "You mean . . . *you're* the one who invents the cookie recipes?" It couldn't be. Could it? "*Not* your dad?"

Flynn blew out a weighty breath. "I figured this would happen
eventually. Somebody outside the shop would find out. And—
you know what?—it feels good. *Finally*, somebody else knows
the truth!" His face broke into a relieved smile that was so unexpected, I was helpless to do anything but sink onto another stool
beside him. Forgetting, for the moment, that only last night, I'd
vowed never to speak to him again and sworn him off as a rude
jerk, I stared at him, mystified.

"How?" I finally managed to ask.

Flynn hesitated, seeming to consider how much he wanted to
tell me. When he started talking, his tone was calmer and more
genuine than I'd heard it since I started working at the shop. "I
taught myself to bake when I was around six." Absently, he drew
circles with his fingertip on the flour-dusted countertop. "Back
then, my dad was a chef in Seattle. He was good, but he wanted
to be the best. The five-star kind. But my mom hated that he
worked such long hours. Sometimes, he wouldn't make it home

until almost sunrise." He shrugged. "They fought about it all the time, and eventually, Mom left. After the divorce, my dad would bring me to the restaurant to keep an eye on me. I'd be in the kitchen on the iPad while he prepped dinners. One day, I came across *That's the Way the Cookie Crumbles* . . ."

"I loved that show, too," I said, remembering the reality show sponsored by Cookie Crumbles, where people were given over-the-top cookie recipes to bake.

He nodded, smiling. "I was a goner. It was the only show I'd watch. And then I started trying to bake the recipes while I watched the show. Dad would be cooking dinner entrées, and I'd be there mixing cookie dough, wreaking havoc with a spatula."

I laughed. It was strange, but Flynn's whole face had taken on a different cast now. All its recent hardness was gone, replaced by an appealing vulnerability. I liked seeing him this way, without his defensive edge. I could picture him as a little kid, too, with unkempt auburn curls and a look of intense concentration on his face as he stood on tiptoe to mix cookie dough. "So your dad must've gotten into baking then, too?"

Flynn looked uncomfortable. "Not exactly. Baking was never his forte. He could make these amazing savory dishes but was at a loss when it came to desserts. Anyway, the owner of the restaurant fired him. She said she needed a head chef who could work long hours without a kid in tow." His expression was pained. "Dad guessed he was never going to make it as one of the world's finest chefs. He caught on to the fact I could really bake right around the time he inherited my grandma's old diner here in Oyster Cove." He gestured to the walls of the kitchen.

"Which became A Batch Made in Heaven," I guessed.

"And Dad finally got his chance to shine in the culinary spotlight . . . with the cookies." Flynn's voice was quiet now and held an undercurrent of weary frustration. "The only thing was . . . the cookie recipes weren't—aren't—his. They're mine."

I studied his face, and a wave of compassion passed through me. So much of Flynn's behavior made sense now—his bouts of defensiveness, his reluctance to let me help. No wonder he hadn't wanted someone new to work at the shop, let alone pass the Cookie Challenge.

"But . . . why keep it a secret that you're the one behind the recipes?" I asked.

Flynn's glance fell on the trays of cookie dough waiting to be slid into the oven. "Dad always told me he wanted to protect me from fame. I was young, and he didn't want it to overwhelm my childhood. He used his name on our advertising to give me a fame-free life. Only . . ." His voice dropped away.

"It wasn't just about protecting you?" I asked gently.

He shook his head. "Now that I'm older, I see that a lot of what he did he did so he could promote himself. It wasn't about me . . . not the way he tried to tell me it was."

Another thought struck me. "How does it work? Keeping the secret?"

"It's not that hard, really." He gestured to his notebook. "I keep my recipe book locked up unless I'm using it. Hughie is the only one who's closest to knowing the whole truth. He knows that I help Dad with the recipes, but he still doesn't realize that I invent them alone. Dad and I mix all the dough ahead of time so Hughie and Stella don't know what goes into it. They help bake the cookies, but they never know all the ingredients we use."

"I knew there was something fishy going on!" I blurted with some satisfaction. Then I instantly felt guilty over what had come out sounding like gloating. I backtracked. "But you have such an amazing setup!" I took in the beautiful kitchen, with its four enormous ovens, stand mixer, and rows of tall multilevel baking racks. "I mean, if I had a kitchen like this, I'd never leave it."

"Don't be so sure." His face tightened. "It's not that great."

"But you love baking," I pointed out.

"*Used* to love baking." He frowned. "Now it's just a job."

"*Just* a job?" I repeated incredulously. "The best job ever." He scowled, and I threw up my hands. "You're so lucky, and you don't even see it."

"Lucky that I'm in this shop every morning, and every day after school, when all my friends are . . . ?" He turned away. "Forget it. I knew you wouldn't understand."

"You're right. I don't." I stared at him. "If you don't want to be here, why not just tell your dad?"

"Never gonna happen." He stood up, avoiding my gaze as he slid the cookie trays into the oven. "The shop is so popular. Dad needs me to keep making the recipes. And if the truth came out, his reputation would be ruined. The whole shop would crater."

"It wouldn't—"

"Stop," Flynn said, closing the oven door. "Just stop. You don't have all the answers, so don't act like you do."

I sucked in a breath, my cheeks burning. "I wasn't! I—"

"It's not your problem." He didn't face me, and I wondered if he was expecting me to leave.

Instead, I planted my hands on my hips. "Actually, it is. Because if we're going to work together, I need you to drop the attitude."

"We're not going to work together." He finally glanced back at me. "You quit last night, remember?"

"I came here to prove you wrong. I was going to convince your dad to let me bake for him and demand a second chance at the Cookie Challenge."

Flynn frowned. "That's not a good idea—"

"Why not?" I demanded as a new idea took hold. "You don't have to hide your secret from me anymore. I could help you with recipes and then you wouldn't feel so burned out about baking." My words tumbled out in a torrent.

Flynn gave me a long look. "Keeping this secret makes it hard for me to make new friends. Trust isn't something that comes easily to me."

"Well, trust is the only way to have real friendships," I stated matter-of-factly. "So, I want a shot at baking my best. I deserve it."

He laughed despite himself, throwing up his hands. "I guess I can't say no. If I did, you'd spill my secret."

I glared at him. "I wouldn't. Not ever. This isn't me bribing you. This is me telling you to give this idea a try."

I held my breath while he considered this. At last, he said, "Okay. I'll choose the ingredients. You'll bake. The Cookie

Challenge is on." He extended his hand for us to shake on it, and I slid my fingers into his.

There it was again, a tingling zing of electricity shooting from my fingertips straight to my heart. I ducked my head to hide the sudden flush I felt in my cheeks.

Thankfully, Flynn didn't seem to notice my blush. He led me into the kitchen's huge pantry. Wow. There were canisters that held candies, and Oreos, marshmallows, caramels, and baking chocolate in a variety of flavors and colors. There were also containers of crushed lavender, rose petals, dried orange slices, and more. I wondered what Flynn would choose. I watched him grab a container of colorful, icing-covered animal cookies, plus a canister of white chocolate bits. Next, he headed to the fridge, where he removed a strawberry cheesecake.

He set everything on the counter, along with all the classic baking staples of sugar, butter, flour, and eggs. Next, Flynn removed his beautiful batches of cookies from the oven, then settled onto a stool to watch me work.

"You may begin," he announced.

I held up a finger of warning. "No comments. No criticism." I wagged my finger. "Not one word until you taste the cookies."

He nodded, and his eyes glinted with amusement at my orders. I made a mental note *not* to look him in the eyes again until I was finished baking. They were *way* too distracting. My heart doubled its pace. I couldn't blow my second shot. I wouldn't.

I reviewed the ingredients, thinking for a moment, and then inspiration struck. I got to work, chopping the animal crackers into chunky pieces. I didn't want them to be too small, because that would ruin their fun effect.

At first, I was acutely aware of Flynn's eyes following my every move. I caught him perched on the edge of his stool, as if he were dying to leap off it to interrupt me with a suggestion or criticism. He was true to his word, though, and kept silent. Soon, as I got lost in the rhythm of measuring out ingredients and mixing butter, sugar, and eggs in the giant stand mixer, I forgot about Flynn's presence entirely.

I blended up a batch of creamy dough and then gently stirred in the animal cookies and white chocolate chips. I dropped generous mounds of dough onto a cookie sheet, then pressed a spoon into the top of each mound to create a crater in the middle. Then I set a square of strawberry cheesecake into each crater and pressed the dough over the top. In the end, the cookie dough sat in happy little hilltops on the sheet, dotted with pastel colors. I slid the trays into the oven and set the timer.

"Come on," I said to Flynn, then, "I'll help you open the shop while the cookies bake."

I thought he might protest, but he seemed grateful for the help. When we walked out of the Cookie Vault, we saw that Mr. Winston and Hughie had both arrived. Hughie's mouth formed a perfect O when he saw me while Mr. Winston folded his arms across his chest, eyeing both of us suspiciously.

"Don't worry, Dad," Flynn said quickly before Mr. Winston even had a chance to speak. "Mina's just taking the Cookie Challenge. That's all." Flynn shot me a quick side glance that clearly meant I shouldn't mention anything about the big secret. I gave him a slight nod to show I understood.

Mr. Winston's expression was dubious, but Hughie clasped his hands together. "A new baker in the kitchen!" he cried jubilantly. "It's our lucky day."

"We'll see" came Flynn's cryptic response. My elbow shot out, catching him in the ribs, and he yelped. "What? You still haven't passed the test."

"I *will*."

He grunted but smiled. "Come on," he said. "We have work to do."

We set Flynn's latest batch of cookies into the display racks and flipped the sign on the door back to OPEN as the first customers of the day arrived. I'd just handed a cookie to a customer when my phone's timer buzzed.

Flynn and I looked at each other, knowing what that meant. Flynn tried to beat me into the kitchen, but I maneuvered past him, announcing, "They're *my* cookies. I get to take them out of the oven."

"But *I* get to taste them first," he countered, perching on his stool.

My heart hummed happily as I discovered the cookies had baked into perfectly golden mountains of pastel colors and delectable white chocolate chips. None of the cheesecake had oozed through the dough, which meant the cookie centers would offer a secret surprise to everyone eating them.

"They're beautiful." Flynn wasn't able to mask the surprise in his voice.

I raised an eyebrow at him. "I expected nothing less." The cookies were still hot and soft. I carefully slid a spatula under one of the prettiest and set it on a plate.

"Go ahead." I put the plate before him. "I dare you."

My stomach tightened as Flynn blew on the cookie and lifted it to his mouth. *This was it.*

I scooped up a cookie of my own. The second I bit into it, I knew I'd succeeded. The sweet crunch of the animal cookies combined with the creamy, rich cheesecake center made for an exciting and fun texture. And the taste! I closed my eyes and smiled.

When I opened them again, I found Flynn staring at me, his cheeks puffed like a chipmunk's with cookies.

"They're okay," he said casually.

I arched my eyebrow. "They're way better than okay. Admit it."

He finally gave a relinquishing nod as he swallowed. "They're delicious."

I crossed my arms. "There. Was that so hard to say?"

"Painful." He grinned. "But true."

"You're impossible." I laughed. "So . . . I'm in?"

He slowly nodded. "You're in."

"Yes!" I squealed, performing a little happy dance. Flynn rolled his eyes, but he laughed.

"What should we call these?" he asked, examining the cookies.

"How about . . . Cheesecake and Chill?" I suggested.

"Catchy." He bit into another cookie.

I smiled. "Working with you will be a challenge if you eat all our products."

"I love a challenge," he said, and my heart stuttered out its own version of *Me too*.

He started for a third cookie, but I slid the tray beyond his reach, and his groan of disappointment made me laugh all over again. "You can have another one in a minute," I conceded. "I have a favor to ask first."

He looked wary. "I thought letting you help me in the Cookie Vault *was* the favor."

I shook my head. "Nope. That's what my mentorship was supposed to be, remember?"

"I guess," he conceded.

"Here's the thing," I said. "I promised to keep your secret, and I will. And in return, I'd like your help."

"With what?"

I took a deep breath, then told him about my plan to enter the Cookie Crumbles competition. "I need to use the Cookie Vault to invent a recipe so out of this world that it will win. It's too hard for me to focus at home."

Flynn thought this over. "It's a nationwide contest. I'm surprised you'd even want to enter it. I wouldn't."

"*You* wouldn't because you're completely burned out," I countered. "*I'm* not."

"True," he admitted. "But winning would be a total long shot."

"Maybe." I nodded. "But I have to try. My dad's dreamed of opening a restaurant for so long. I want to do this for my family."

Flynn's brow creased. "My dad had that dream once, too, remember? I've been down that road." His voice held a bitter edge. "What we ended up with instead was this time suck of a shop."

I stiffened. "You don't mean that. You said you loved inventing recipes."

"Loved. Past tense." He turned away. "My whole life revolves around this shop. That's never what I wanted."

"What do you want, then?" I challenged.

He blew out a breath. "I don't know! A break. Time to try other things." He shook his head. "Forget it. You don't want to hear this."

Suddenly, I felt like the ground we'd gained over the last couple of hours was slipping away all over again. The second I felt I was breaking down Flynn's defenses, they shot back up again. Somehow, I always ended up saying the wrong thing. *Doing* the wrong thing.

"But—"

He held up a hand. "Use the Cookie Vault. That's fine. I'll make sure it's cool with my dad. Just . . . don't let it take over your whole life."

Then he walked through the kitchen door, leaving me reeling and wondering if he'd ever actually let down his guard enough for us to become friends.

Chapter Six

"Apple pie filling in a cookie?" Flynn raised an eyebrow at me, leaning back against the counter. "Are you sure?"

I'd come to recognize this look as quintessential Flynn. It didn't unnerve me; it only made me want to rise to his challenge.

I grinned defiantly, then turned back to mixing the diced apples, sugar, and cinnamon.

Over the past week, I'd stopped into Batch after school almost every day to work on recipes in the Cookie Vault. I'd spent most of Saturday and Sunday experimenting there, too.

I'd made You're My Butter Half jelly-stuffed peanut butter cookies, Mellow Out marshmallow-stuffed cookies coated with chocolate icing, and more.

As long as I helped with the shop's regular baking, too, Mr. Winston didn't mind me using the Vault's ovens. Hughie and Stella were grateful for the extra pair of helping hands, too. Flynn, though, watched my baking experiments unfold with a skepticism that was so infuriating, it only served to fuel my determination.

"You mind your own business," I said with mock sternness now, jabbing my spatula at the bowl of Cookie Monster dough in his hands. "You're supposed to be worrying about your own batch, remember?"

He sighed, glancing down at the bowl. "I never thought I'd actually come to hate this cookie. It used to be my favorite."

"Really?" I paused to glance up from adding dollops of pie filling to the centers of the sugar cookie dough balls on my tray. The sugar-cinnamon apple mixture would be spooned over caramel squares, which I hoped would meld together during baking to form the perfect blend of caramel-apple sweetness. "Why was it your favorite?"

"It was the first cookie I ever tried baking." He shrugged. "I raided our pantry, and it turned into a free-for-all and an accidental success."

"The cookie that started it all?" I asked, and he nodded.

Then his cell phone buzzed. He glanced down at a text message on his screen, and a shadow crossed his face. He shoved his phone into his back pocket without responding to it.

"Maybe I should take over the baking for a bit," I offered a few minutes later, after he'd absentmindedly burned a batch of Cookie Monsters and his scowl still hadn't disappeared.

"Why?" he blurted in an accusatory tone.

"Because you've been in a funk ever since you got that text," I countered. "You're completely zoned out. What's the deal?"

"Nothing." But when I folded my arms, indicating I wasn't buying it, his shoulders sagged. "Trent and Will just won their archery tournament. They're down the street at Buona Notte's Pizza celebrating."

The bitterness in his voice was barely masked, but there was a yearning underneath it, too. "You could meet them," I offered, guessing that was what he really wanted. "I can cover for you here."

Flynn shook his head. "Did you see the line of customers out front? We're swamped."

I peeked out of the Vault to see Hughie and Mr. Winston behind the sales counter, deftly handling orders without missing a beat. "Oh, wow, yeah. Look at them. *Completely* panicked." I pressed a hand melodramatically to my forehead. "How *ever* will we handle the shop without you?"

"Very funny." He gave a short laugh, then grew serious. "You don't get it. I can't just go hang with Trent and Will right now. The whole archery team's there, and I'm—"

"Not on it?" I finished for him, mentally filling in the missing piece of the puzzle. "And you feel like the odd man out."

His cheeks flushed. "I never said that," he mumbled.

"What about joining the team?" I asked, removing my batch of apple cookies from the oven.

"That'll never happen. Practices are every day after school during archery season. That'll never fly with Dad."

"Have you asked him?"

His silence was the only response I needed.

"Do you like archery?" I pressed.

He shrugged. "I've never had the time to try it. Or anything else, really, besides baking. I'm always working here."

I studied his face with fresh interest. Was this why he was so edgy? Because he felt like he had no life outside the shop? My fix-it brain shifted into high gear, and suddenly, inspiration struck.

"*You* need a break from baking monotony, and *I* have an idea." I pulled off my apron and swung open the door to the Vault, calling over my shoulder, "Be ready to go in ten minutes!"

"A boat?" Flynn asked incredulously. He stared at *Akshiti*, my family's little sailboat, as she bobbed up and down in the Oyster Cove harbor.

"She's a skiff," I said matter-of-factly, relishing his expression of complete discombobulation. "My family's. My dad learned how to sail when he moved here from India. He grew up in a landlocked city, but when he came to Oyster Cove, he fell in love with the water. He taught me to sail, too. And now *you're* going to learn how today."

"Wha— Nope." He shook his head adamantly. "I've never even been on the Sound . . ."

I'd been busying myself with raising the sail but now stopped to stare at him. "You're kidding, right? You've lived here for how long, and you've never been on the Sound?"

"Six years, and I told you—I've never had time to do stuff like this."

"Well, no time like the present." I tossed him a life jacket. "How are you ever going to figure out what you're into if you don't try something besides baking?" He huffed, but I didn't give up. "Hate me all you want to. Just get in the boat!"

After a few seconds' stare-down, Flynn climbed into the boat on unsteady legs. "I don't hate you," he mumbled softly. But he was wearing such a ridiculously pouty expression that I couldn't help but laugh.

"Who knows? Sailing could be your life's calling." I gave Flynn a quick tour of our boat, naming all the parts and explaining the basics of sailing in the simplest terms I could. Flynn sat down, and I raised the anchor. I guided the boat smoothly over the calm waters and out into Whaler's Cove, then tilted my face back to relish the full force of the cool breeze against my skin.

"Isn't it beautiful?" I said, sweeping my hand across the view stretching out before us. It had been months since I'd been on the boat, and it felt exhilarating. Next to baking, sailing was one of my favorite things to do. Of course, sailing with Dad was even better, but who knew when he'd have time for it again? For now, I'd enjoy this day, this moment, and try to make sure Flynn enjoyed it, too.

The windows of the town's hillside houses caught the afternoon light, glittering gold. From the water, our Main Street, with its lovely, colorful, canopied shops and outdoor cafés, looked picture-perfect, like something out of an old Norman Rockwell painting. Autumn mums were planted in window boxes and hanging from the old-fashioned lampposts lining the street. Shoppers strolled leisurely past the stores and harbor, coffees in one hand, bags in the other.

"I love seeing our town from the water," I said, "with everything in miniature. And out here, the sky breaks wide open, and the view of the mountains is just . . . wow."

When Flynn didn't respond, I looked at him, about to chide him for not enjoying the view. But the words fell away when I caught his gaze focused on my face. A small smile played around his lips, and his expression looked almost . . . charmed. But that was impossible when we'd barely even achieved frenemy status. Still, his expression made warmth flood through me. Our eyes met, and he looked away, clearing his throat awkwardly.

"I can't believe my dad agreed to this," he muttered.

And the old Flynn is back, I thought, giving myself a reality check.

"Well, it was actually more Hughie than your dad," I said. When I'd asked him if Flynn could have the afternoon off,

Hughie didn't even hesitate and was thrilled when I told him about my sailing idea.

"If anybody needs a healthy dose of blue mind, it's that boy," Hughie had said with delight. "Bon voyage to the both of you!" Mr. Winston's feelings about the idea had been more difficult to read, but after I offered to make all the cookie deliveries on the way to the boat, he'd agreed.

"Hughie and Stella are helping your dad," I assured Flynn now. "I handled everything."

Flynn laughed softly as he settled his gaze on the islands in the distance. "Are you always so convinced that you have the answers to everything?" he asked.

"No, of course not," I protested, but when he challenged me with his eyes, I shrugged. "Maybe . . . a little."

"And how does that work out?"

"Usually fine," I said confidently. "I'm pretty good at fixing problems. At least, my friends tell me I am." Then I reached into the bottom of the boat and held up the one remaining Batch

Made in Heaven delivery bag. "Speaking of problems, in this very bag might be the solution to my recipe problem."

"For the Cookie Crumbles competition?" Flynn asked.

I nodded. "Time to taste-test." I pulled the last two cookies from the bag and held one out to him. We bit into the cookies almost at the same time. Just as I'd hoped, the apple-caramel combo had melted into a beautifully gooey center. Along with the cinnamon and butterscotch morsels in the dough, the rich center made the cookie mouthwateringly amazing.

"Mmmmm," I said around my mouthful.

Flynn nodded. "Yup. This could be it."

I took a second bite, contemplating. "It's delicious. But . . . not quite right."

"Mina, you have to submit an entry in two days. The deadline is Friday, and you—"

"Still haven't decided on one." I sighed. "I know, I know." Each recipe I'd come up with so far had been delicious, but I needed something *more* than just delicious. I needed a cookie that was out-of-this-world, knock-your-socks-off spectacular. I couldn't put my finger on exactly what it was that was making me so hesitant to decide on a recipe. All I knew was that none of the recipes I'd invented over the last six days had been "wow"-worthy.

"I want to bake the perfect batch," I said now. "When I taste it, I'll know."

"Love at first bite?" Flynn said teasingly, but the playful words made my cheeks flame. "You have impossible standards."

I stared at him, then burst out laughing. "Me? Look who's talking! You failed me in the Cookie Challenge *before* I even baked anything!"

"Okay. I'll give you that." He laughed, then quieted. "This Cookie Crumbles competition . . . why is it so important to you?" he asked. "You think it will fix your family? That if you give your dad what he needs to run a restaurant, everything will be perfect?"

"No," I protested. "My family doesn't need fixing. We're fine." I squirmed uncomfortably, knowing my words rang insincere. I refused to look at Flynn, focusing on my steering instead. I

adjusted the tiller slightly, and the boat's sail snapped and bal-
looned, filling with the breeze. I hoped Flynn would let the
subject drop, but of course, he called my bluff, seeing right
through my pretense.

"Nuh-uh." He shook his head. "Not buying it."

I huffed out a breath. *"Okay,"* I relented. "We're not totally
fine. My parents are exhausted with the twins. Every time I
look at them, *I* feel guilty. Like maybe I should be doing more to
help. But then I get angry because I already help a ton, and they
don't even see it." With a simmering frustration, I told Flynn
about how I'd given up going to the movies this past Saturday
with Kalli, Jane, and Fabiana so that I could babysit the twins
while my parents went out for a quick bite to eat. "It's not fair for
me to have so much responsibility."

"Have you talked to them about it?" he asked.

I swallowed hard. "That's the weird thing. I used to be a
complete oversharer with my dad. But I can't speak up right
now . . . They're already dealing with so much. I don't need to
add to their problems."

Flynn stared out at the water thoughtfully. "You're not a problem. You're their daughter." My stomach knotted. I felt exposed by what he'd said, like he'd uncovered this vulnerable side of me that I didn't like showing anyone. He must've sensed that he'd thrown me off balance, because he added, "I get it, though. I don't talk to my dad about heavy stuff, either."

"Have you even told him that I know about you and the recipes?"

Flynn shook his head. "Are you kidding? No way. He'd freak. He got burned by my mom pretty badly. It's a good thing she lives halfway across the country. They can't stand each other. And, well, he doesn't want anybody to see the man behind the curtain, you know?"

I nodded. "So that's why *you're* on the defensive when you're at the shop?"

He shrugged as he mulled over the question. "It was never intentional. Dad and I were keeping this big secret, and when I was younger, I worried about accidentally letting it slip. I was always on my guard, and I guess it became a habit."

"Sounds exhausting," I said.

"Seriously. But the alternative . . ." His voice died.

I nodded, understanding everything he couldn't say—the burden of the responsibility he felt. "You've had to give up a lot," I said quietly.

He didn't agree or disagree, but his expression drew in on itself, as if he were lost in his own thoughts. I didn't push him to say more, just sat with him in companionable silence.

As I directed the boat into deeper water to get a better view of the San Juan archipelago, I marveled at how my impressions of Flynn were slowly starting to change. I was discovering that we had more in common than I'd originally thought. We both felt intensely loyal to our families but at the same time frustrated by our obligations.

"Okay," I said after we'd circled one of the smallest islands and I'd turned the boat back toward the harbor. "Your turn to take the helm."

"No way." He shook his head adamantly.

"Flynn." I gave him a no-nonsense look. "Don't take this the wrong way, but you need to get a life." He frowned, and I clarified, "A life outside the shop!"

He scoffed, but I persisted. "Come on. You've never been on the Sound until now, and I'm betting there are tons of other things you've been missing out on. Your whole existence centers on the shop, but that ends today." I threw up a hand, like I was making a speech. "Today, we embark on a mission to find your heartsease." At his blank look, I explained, "Something that gives you inner peace. Happiness."

He opened his mouth to argue, I was sure, but before he could, I stood up, removing my hand from the tiller. The boat rocked, but because I'd earned my sea legs years before, I kept my balance.

"What are you doing?" Flynn cried.

"Waiting for you." I held up both my hands. "This boat can't sail itself. We'll just drift aimlessly, probably get lost somewhere in the Pacific, never to be found—"

Flynn stood up without warning, and the boat tilted precariously to one side as we both struggled to keep our balance.

Flynn's arms windmilled wildly as he started to tip over the side, and I grabbed his life jacket to pull him back. The next thing I knew, his arms were wrapped around my waist, and my face was inadvertently pressed into his neck. And—oh my gosh—the cinnamon, fresh-baked-cookie scent lingering on his shirt made me want to stay there, just like that, breathing it in. For a second, I forgot where we were and what we were doing. Every atom in my being was focused on his nearness.

Then a huge spray of water caught the side of the seesawing boat, splashing both of us in the face.

The water's freezing cold sucked my breath away, Flynn hollered, and we both sat down with a hard *thump* on the boat's bench. I glanced at Flynn, whose waterlogged curls were covering his drenched face. He parted his hair like a curtain to grimace in my direction, and then we burst out laughing.

"That went well," he groused, still laughing.

Breathless from my own laughter, I stood up and motioned for him to follow me to the tiller. "Let's try that again. Come here. *Slowly*."

Once we were seated with the tiller between us, I placed his hand on the tiller and then slid mine over his.

"Gently," I said. "The smallest movements make a huge difference."

His hand relaxed under mine, and our fingers warmed against each other. A thrill ran through me, but I removed my hand from his as he put the boat on a course toward shore.

"You're getting the hang of it," I told him as he steered into the harbor. But he seemed relieved when it was time for me to take over to dock the boat.

"So what do you think?" I asked him as I dropped the anchor. "Ready to sail the seven seas?"

"Not quite." He smirked. "Not unless you do the navigating, Captain."

"Ooooh." I straightened my shoulders. "Captain. I like the sound of that."

He snorted. "Don't let it go to your head." He nudged my shoulder with his.

"Better watch it or I'll throw you overboard for mutiny," I teased, nudging him back. He grabbed me around the waist and lifted me off my feet while I shrieked with laughter.

"Mina?" a familiar voice called out, and Flynn put me down, his cheeks reddening.

I glanced up to see Kalli peering at Flynn and me from the end of the dock.

"Kalli! Hey! I just took Flynn on his first sailboat ride ever."

"And she almost drowned me," Flynn teased, and I responded by elbowing him in the ribs, making him yelp in feigned pain. Then I noticed Kalli wasn't joining in our laughter. In fact, she looked stressed.

"Are you okay?" I asked as we climbed off the boat and joined her.

She shook her head. "I'm completely freaking. I texted you a dozen times today and didn't hear back."

"I don't know how I missed your text . . ." My voice trailed off as I realized that I hadn't looked at my phone since we boarded the boat. I glanced at the screen now to see a string of missed texts, not just from her, but from my dad, asking me to pick up takeout from Buona Notte's on the way home. "I'm sorry." I smiled apologetically at Kalli. "I haven't checked my phone in a while."

Kalli didn't look completely convinced. The fact was, I hadn't seen her outside school all week. I'd been so focused on inventing recipes, I'd been distracted whenever we were together with Jane and Fabiana. "I went looking for you at the shop," she continued. "Hughie said you took the boat out, so I came here." She swallowed, fanning herself with her hands. "Ugh . . . I feel sick just thinking about it."

"Thinking about what?" I asked. "The boat?"

She groaned, closing her eyes. "No. The museum wants me to give a living history presentation. Next Tuesday after school. To talk about the impact of Native American cultures on our region."

"Oh!" I said. "That sounds great!"

"Except I *hate* speaking in front of people. I'll forget what I want to say, and I'll freeze, or—or—"

"You just need to practice, that's all." I gave her a confident nod. "Practice until you can give the presentation in your sleep. I'll help you. No problem."

"But you're already busy with your Cookie Crumbles stuff," she pointed out. "And you want to keep everything hush-hush." My heart squeezed with guilt. I'd told Kalli that I passed Mr. Winston's Cookie Vault challenge but had kept the details cryptic so that the shop's secret recipes would never come up. I didn't want her asking questions that I'd have to lie to answer. I didn't like keeping secrets from her, but I couldn't betray Flynn's trust, either. I was walking a tightrope of ambiguity, but I was sure if Kalli were in my position, she'd do the same.

"We'll figure it out," I promised. "I'll make time. You'll be fine." A rare look of exasperation passed over Kalli's face, surprising me. "Hey . . . are you okay? You seem a little . . ." *Angry* was what I was thinking but didn't get the chance to say.

"I'm fine," she said in a clipped voice, then checked her phone. "I'm meeting Fabs at her house to study for our Spanish test, so I better get going."

"I'll call you tonight," I promised. A prick of remorse stung me as I watched her wave over her shoulder and disappear down the sidewalk. Usually, Kalli and I were in sync, but the last few minutes with her had felt uncharacteristically awkward. As Flynn and I turned toward Main Street, I made a mental note to make sure I called her later.

But my unsettled feeling fled as Flynn offered up a game of Name That Ingredient on the walk through town. He started off describing a spice by flavor and texture and then offering a list of cookies it might be used in. We played four rounds before he held up his hands, laughing.

"I surrender," he said. "You've won every round."

I giggled. "Well, I *did* use the Indian names for some of the spices, just to make it more challenging."

"Oh, I'll be ready for round two." He grinned. "You can bet on it."

As we reached Batch, Flynn stopped walking to face me.

My heart fluttered. Being around Flynn today had felt so different. It wasn't just our conversation. *He* was different—more open, honest, and relaxed. This side of him was refreshing and . . . charming. It was a realization that confused me and made me hyperaware of his eyes on mine now.

"Hey," he said quietly. "Um, thanks. For today." The dusky, late-afternoon sky nearly matched his eyes, and I felt a sudden light-headedness. "It was fun. I would never have taken the afternoon off if—"

"If I hadn't forced you?" I teased.

He laughed. "It *was* because of you. You're very—"

"Pushy?" I offered.

He shook his head, grinning. "I was going to say 'persistent.' But 'pushy' works, too!" I glared at him, but he only laughed again. "'Pushy' . . . in the best way."

My cheeks flamed. "See? I've become indispensable. You can't run the shop without me," I joked. "I knew it."

"Don't push your luck." He smirked. "But I'm glad you're working at the shop. Really, I am."

I smiled. "Me too."

Our eyes locked for a split second, and then Flynn fumbled for the door. Warmth filled me as I walked away. My mind reasoned that it was because of windburn from our boat ride. But my heart beat out a happy rhythm as I thought back on Flynn's words.

Chapter Seven

Because of you. Those three words singsonged through my head as I set the cartons of Buona Notte pasta on the kitchen counter. I popped open the container of marinara sauce and began to pour, when Dad's voice jolted me from my thoughts.

"Mina!" He clucked his tongue. "Were you planning on drinking that?"

"Huh?" I glanced down to see I'd poured part of the red sauce into my water cup. "Oh!" I blushed as I poured out the mess in the cup. "I guess I'm a little distracted."

"A little?" Mom said. She was pacing the length of the kitchen with Amul tucked against her shoulder, patting his back as he gurgled. "I worry about you, beti."

"I'm fine," I said, ducking my head and focusing on plating the pasta. But my parents didn't buy it.

"First, you sail the boat without telling us." Dad's gaze was somber.

"I *did* tell you!" I argued for what felt like the hundredth time. "I called and left you two messages. You never called me back, and I've gone out by myself before dozens of times, so I knew it was okay."

Dad huffed. "And you spent all weekend at that cookie shop . . . I have a mind to call Mr. Winston to discuss this. You're far too young to be working such long hours."

"You can't call him!" I blurted with such force that both my parents looked up in surprise.

I'd let my parents continue thinking that each time I went to the shop, I was "working" for Mr. Winston when really I was working on the contest. But I already suspected that Mr. Winston wasn't keen on my baking alongside Flynn. If my parents called him, Mr. Winston might agree with them and tell me that I couldn't come into the shop whenever I wanted anymore.

I *couldn't* lose the gift of being able to bake in the Cookie Vault. I hadn't even decided on my recipe for the Cookie Crumbles contest.

"I mean . . ." I gazed at my parents' startled faces. "I love working at the shop. I'm keeping up with my studies, and Mr. Winston needs the help . . ."

Dad waved a hand. "You've always been a good student, beti. It's not that." He rubbed his forehead. "We need your help *here*. With your sister and brother."

"I *am* helping," I said. As if to prove a point, after I set the filled plates on the table, I scooped up Banita from her rocker and blew a raspberry into her chubby belly. She let out a drooly coo of contentment.

"Yes, we know." Mom pressed her hand against my cheek, and I leaned into it gladly. I might've been too old for the doting cuddles she gave my brother and sister, but I realized that it seemed like months since Mom had really noticed me. She turned away, though, and the moment ended all too soon. "But *where* is your head these days? You've been forgetting your chores, not answering our calls and texts."

Dad nodded. "Your mother and I have a lot on our minds. We need to be able to count on you. If that means cutting back on this baking mentorship—"

"No!" Panic rose in my throat. "I'll help more." I stared them down stubbornly. "I'll make it work."

They exchanged uncertain glances, but finally, my mom said, "All right, Mina. But you have to do better with checking in with us. And I don't want to find any more dirty dishes left in the sink or laundry tossed on the floor of your room." She offered me a tired smile. "Soon the babies won't need us quite as much. But until then, we all need to pitch in."

Frustration burbled inside me. How could my parents be accusing me of not working hard enough when all I did from the second I came home was work? How many of my friends spent their evenings changing diapers, rinsing out burp cloths, and doing laundry? *None*, I thought. Kalli had three older brothers, and Fabs and Jane had younger sisters only a grade level below them. These days, I felt more like a babysitter than a regular kid. But if that was what was going to get our family through this rough patch, then that's what I had to keep doing.

"I'll do better," I said now, pushing my frustrations down deeper. "I promise."

"Mina?" Kalli's voice was a distant buzz in my ear as I stared down at my recipe journal. The page was riddled with crossed-out ingredients, telltale signs of my "baker's block." I'd gone upstairs after dinner to call Kalli, but I'd made the mistake of opening my recipe journal at the same time.

"Mina!" This time, Kalli's voice was loud and insistent enough to break through my daze.

"Sorry!" I readjusted my phone against my ear. "I'm here!"

"You were totally spacing." Kalli's voice was heavy with disappointment.

"I was listening." I frowned at the recipe book in my lap,

tempted to launch it across the room. "You were talking about your presentation."

"No." Kalli sighed. "I wasn't. I asked what was up with you and Flynn."

Heat pricked my cheeks at the mention of his name. "What do you mean? Nothing's *up* with us."

"Really? Because my flirt radar was pinging like crazy when I saw you two at the docks today."

"We weren't flirting!" I protested. But *had* we been flirting? It kind of felt like we had. It also felt like I was having trouble concentrating on anything but Flynn today. I shook that thought from my brain to focus on Kalli. "Flynn doesn't have a life outside the shop," I explained, "so I wanted him to try sailing, that's all. To say thank you for helping me with my contest recipes."

"Wait . . . *He's* helping you with your recipes?" Kalli's tone was doubtful. "I thought recipes were his dad's specialty."

"They—they are!" I stammered. How could I have made a slip like that? "I meant that Flynn's been helping me with the baking part." I gripped the phone tightly, hoping that would be enough to quell Kalli's questions.

There was a long silence. "Okay," Kalli said. "Whatever. It's obvious you don't want to tell me about it. So fine."

I cringed. Kalli *did* know me. *So* well. Of course she'd sense my evasiveness. "It's not that. Really." It hurt me to say it. I'd never kept a secret from her before, and it didn't feel right. My stomach churned uneasily. "I'm stuck on ideas for the contest recipe. That's why I'm so distracted. Things are just a little complicated with me right now."

She let out a short laugh. "And they're not for *me*? I'm about to do something that's completely out of my comfort zone, and I'm petrified."

"But you don't have to be!" I said. "I'll make sure of it."

"Mina." There was that exasperation again. "There's no way you can make sure that something bad won't happen. And you can't talk me out of feeling scared. Because *I'm* the one feeling it. Not you. *Me*."

I sat back on my bed, stunned by her words. For the first time I could ever remember, Kalli sounded frustrated with *me*.

"That's not what I meant," I said. "I know they're your feelings. I only want to help." I smiled encouragingly into the phone, as if somehow that might solve everything. "Hey, why don't we practice right now?"

"Actually, I already practiced at Fabiana's house today."

"Oh. Well . . . great! Are you sure you don't want to go through it again? I could give you some pointers. I'll be a rapt audience. Promise."

"Not tonight," she said softly.

My heart sank. Kalli had always turned to me for help. And now she didn't want my help at all. What was happening?

"Maybe we could run through it together before school tomorrow morning?" she offered then. "We could catch up?"

"Sure," I said, relieved. "I'll meet you at the school library?"

"Sounds good."

We said goodbye and hung up. Guilt weighed on my chest like a stone. I'd nearly spilled Flynn's secret to Kalli, after I'd sworn I wouldn't. I'd have to be more careful from now on, especially around Kalli and my other friends. But that meant hiding the truth from my best friends, which only made me feel worse.

I flipped through the pages of my recipe journal, scouring the recipes Dad and I had created over the years, in search of that one ingredient that would make my Cookie Crumbles entry truly stand out from the rest. No luck.

Thinking I might find inspiration in our kitchen spice rack, I opened my bedroom door and nearly slammed straight into my dad. He was standing in the middle of our upstairs hallway, staring at a photo on the wall, so lost in his thoughts he didn't even startle. I could hear the twins crying in the nursery as my mom tried to shush them.

I moved to Dad's side to see the photograph he was looking at. It showed the colorful red-and-yellow exterior of Nilay, Dad's old restaurant in Delhi. *Nilay* was a Hindi word meaning "home." My dad had chosen the name because that's how he wanted customers to feel when they walked through the door, like they were being welcomed home. In the photo, a younger version of my parents stood in front of the restaurant, beaming.

"You miss it," I said to Dad now, studying his wistful expression.

"Yes." His voice was weary. "I miss cooking for customers. I miss giving them the joy of a delicious meal. I thought surely by now . . ."

"That we'd have our restaurant here," I finished for him. "Did you call Mrs. Yang about her space yet? The sign's still up in her window."

"Your mother and I need to speak about it more," he said.

"Why?" I asked in disbelief. I felt a flash of anger at Mom, guessing that it was her reservations about the restaurant that were keeping them from moving ahead.

I'd heard her and Dad arguing about it once when they thought I was asleep. She was ticking off a list of reasons why a restaurant would be too difficult to open. The hours were too long, and it would be too challenging to balance with children. "It was different in Delhi when your family helped run the restaurant, too," she'd said to him. "Here it would just be you and me, and I have my job to consider." What Mom didn't understand was that they'd have my help, too. With everything. I was the solution.

"Doesn't Mom want you to open it?" I asked Dad. "I mean, there's nothing to talk about! This is what you want, and—"

"Mina," he interrupted, reaching for my hand to give it a squeeze. "Sometimes our lives take an unexpected path, but that doesn't mean we don't eventually reach our destination."

"You'll definitely call Mrs. Yang, though," I said, squeezing his hand back, wanting to hear him say it aloud. He didn't. It was on the tip of my tongue to tell him about my plan to win the Cookie Crumbles contest so that he'd understand that he and Mom wouldn't be opening the restaurant alone.

Not yet, I decided. It was too soon to tell him. If I didn't come up with the perfect recipe, I might not win, and there'd be no use getting his hopes up only to disappoint him in the end. Besides, it would be such a wonderful surprise for him when I *did* win. Keeping the secret now would make telling him the news later all the more delicious.

Suddenly, another thought struck me. "Dad," I said. "What was your favorite spice to cook with at Nilay?"

There wasn't even a second's hesitation before he said, "Garam masala spices." He smiled. "My specialty was garam masala chicken curry—the most popular dish in the restaurant."

"Like the one we've made before?" I asked. One of the first curry combination of spices Dad had taught me how to blend was garam masala. It was a spicy blend of pepper, cardamom, cinnamon, cumin, nutmeg, and cloves. It added a savory richness to curry dishes, and I'd always loved its taste.

A flash of inspiration filled me with renewed energy. I *knew* what ingredient had been missing from all my baking attempts so far.

"Dad," I said, "I just realized I forgot something really important at A Batch Made in Heaven. Can I go back to get it?"

He checked his watch and frowned. "At this hour? It's nearly nine o'clock!"

"I'm sorry, but I really need to go. I'll text you when I get there, and I'll come home as soon as I can."

He hesitated but reluctantly nodded.

"Be quick, and keep your phone on." He gave me a serious look. "If I text you or call, you answer right away."

I gave him a thumbs-up, and then I was rushing down the stairs. After grabbing the jar of spices I needed and two bars of Amul dark chocolate from Mom's stash of her favorite Indian-made chocolates, I hurried out the door with my backpack of baking goodies. I texted Flynn as I jogged down the sidewalk.

Can you meet me at Batch asap? I typed. *I think I have the perfect recipe, and I need a taste tester.*

I didn't wait for a reply, only doubled my pace through the starlit streets, hoping Flynn would be waiting for me when I reached the shop.

Fifteen minutes later, I was standing in front of A Batch Made in Heaven's industrial mixer as the eggs and sugar churned into a cheery, creamy swirl in the metal bowl.

"I was talking to my dad and then—*wham!*—there it was!" I grinned at Flynn, who was sitting on the stool at the kitchen counter. "I had it! The perfect ingredient." I turned off the mixture and took the chocolate bars and Dad's spices from my backpack. "My dad's homemade garam masala spices."

Flynn raised an eyebrow. "You're going to use the spices in a cookie recipe?"

The doubt in his voice made me laugh. "No comments until the final taste test."

He bowed. "Your wish is my command, milady."

"Ooooh, careful." I swept past him to scoop some flour from one of the large canisters on the nearby shelf. "I could get used to that." The euphoria that had swept over me back at home lingered, and I hurried around the kitchen, gathering up ingredients in a flurry of excitement. I added flour, baking powder, cocoa powder, and vanilla into the mixer. I was so absorbed in my tasks that I almost forgot about Flynn's presence entirely until he broke into laughter, startling me from my focus. I glanced up to find his eyes glinting, and I blushed, wondering how long he'd been watching me.

"You're practically dancing around the kitchen!" He grinned.

My blush deepened, and an embarrassed giggle popped out of me. "I didn't even realize . . . I guess I'm just on a roll."

"It's great. You're totally inspired. I love it when that happens. Or"—he paused—"I used to, anyway."

I slapped my palms flat onto the counter and leaned toward him with a no-nonsense stare. "Okay. That's it. I'm tired of your moping. And of you being so convinced that you don't enjoy baking anymore. What you need . . . is to fall in love."

The words hung in the air for a second before the realization of what I'd said—and what it might mean—dawned on me. Flynn's cheeks turned pink as heat swept across my own face. *Oh no!* "With baking!" I blurted, my eyes looking everywhere but at him. "You need to fall in love with baking again." My legs felt like they were puddling onto the floor with humiliation.

"You're wrong," Flynn said quietly. "I need to get away from baking and the shop."

"But baking is part of who you are," I argued. "Not all of you, but an important piece. You can't keep denying that."

"Says the girl who thinks she has all the answers."

"Maybe not *all*." I sighed. "For instance, I have no idea why chocolate chip cookies weren't invented until the 1930s. I mean, how did people survive before that?"

That made him laugh, and while his guard was down, I took the opportunity to slap a spatula into his hand. I grabbed my phone and turned on my fave baking playlist—a mash-up of upbeat pop songs I loved to sing along to as I baked. Next, I pulled an empty mixing bowl off the counter and launched it like a Frisbee toward Flynn. He caught it against his stomach, laughing. "I challenge you to a battle of the bakers," I said. "Brand-new cookie recipe, at least one never-before-used ingredient. Whichever new recipe sells the most in the shop tomorrow wins. Deal?" I stuck out my hand toward him, holding my breath as I waited.

He hesitated. "This isn't going to work," he mumbled. But when my hand didn't budge an inch, he finally shook it. "Deal."

"Yes!" I cried jubilantly. "I've got a head start," I added teasingly. "Better get going, slacker."

"Oh, you did *not* just say that." His expression lit with mischief. "It's on!" And with that, he set to work.

For the next half an hour, as music filled the kitchen, we worked side by side, a comfortable, effortless energy whirring between us. When I tried to peek at his cookie batter, he whisked the mixing bowl to the other side of the kitchen while humming the opening chords of the *Mission: Impossible* theme song.

I cracked up. "If your batter is going to self-destruct in ten seconds, we have a serious problem."

"Eyes on your own work, rookie" came his teasing response.

Whenever I snuck a glance at Flynn, I caught a look of satisfied concentration on his face, a purposeful gleam in his eyes. His auburn locks framed his angular cheekbones, and his lips pursed adorably as he focused. His hands were nimble and confident as they sprinkled a dash of this or that into the bowl, without the use of any measuring spoons or cups. Watching Flynn bake was like watching a conductor leading an orchestra—mesmerizing and awe-inspiring all at once.

It was tough to focus on my own recipe when my eyes kept finding their way back to him, but I reminded myself how much was at stake, and at last, my cookies were ready for baking. The mounds of dark brown batter sat in little rows of potential on the tray, but I'd only know if I'd succeeded when I tasted one of the finished cookies. Flynn and I both opened our oven doors at the same moment, nodding at each other with mock seriousness. But just as we were about to slide the cookie trays into the oven, a voice from the dining room called out, "Hello? Anybody here?"

Flynn slapped a hand to his forehead. "I forgot to lock the front door when you came in."

"I'll handle it," I said, not wanting to disrupt Flynn in baking mode. I breezed into the dining room to find an older man scrutinizing the few remaining cookies in the display case.

"I'm sorry," I said breathlessly. "The shop is closed for the night."

He seemed nonplussed. "That's too bad. I was craving cookies, and the door was open."

I nodded, but then my heart gave a sickening lurch. Flynn's

tattered recipe book was lying open on the sales counter. Omigod. He must've put it down when he first came in and then forgot about it.

I swooped toward the counter and, in a flash, grabbed the recipe book, hiding it behind my back. But had this man seen it already? There was no way to know from his benign expression.

"The door shouldn't have been open," I said. "I was just cleaning up for Mr. Winston. Who is . . . um, busy working on tomorrow's Cookie of the Day recipe as we speak."

"Ah." The man nodded, peering at the closed door to the Cookie Vault.

I hurried behind the counter, setting Flynn's recipe book out of sight and snatching up a small to-go box. As far as I was concerned, the sooner this man left the shop, the better. Just in case he *had* seen something and had suspicions. "I'm sorry about the misunderstanding, and as a thank-you for being one of our valued customers . . ." I handed him the box, which I'd quickly filled with leftover cookies. "Here are some cookies. On the house."

He smiled. "Thank you!" He started for the door, giving one last glance toward the Cookie Vault. "Good night."

"Good night," I echoed, locking the front door behind him.

"All okay?" Flynn asked when I returned to the kitchen.

I hesitated. There was no point in sending Flynn into a panic when I was almost sure the man hadn't even noticed the open recipe book. And even if he had seen it, there was no way he would know it belonged to Flynn instead of Mr. Winston, would he?

"All good," I said, quickly slipping the recipe book onto the nearby kitchen counter.

Flynn smiled, then turned his attention back to our waiting cookie trays. "Shall we?"

Grateful to have my mind taken off the close call, I nodded, and we slid our trays into the ovens. After setting the timer, we started cleaning up the kitchen and prepping it for tomorrow's opening. While Flynn got the mop and bucket from the storage closet in the dining room, I turned up the volume on my playlist. I was never allowed to listen to music loudly at home anymore;

Dad always worried it would wake the twins. My fave song began, and I grinned with the relief of being someplace where I could listen to music as loudly as I wanted to. I tapped my toes and began sidestepping in time to the music, mouthing the words to the song as I wiped off the counter.

Suddenly, the Cookie Vault door opened and Flynn slid across the floor, the mop between his hands like a standing microphone. He was dipping the microphone mop, crooning into it and swinging his other arm like he was playing an air guitar.

His ridiculously exaggerated dance moves and goofy expression made me burst out laughing. Then Flynn shot his hand out toward me. I slapped my palm into his, and he spun me around the kitchen, galloping me from one end of the room to the other in a disastrous tango-polka mash-up.

Soon the room was spinning, and I stumbled into him, tripping over my own feet, breathless with laughter. His arms caught my waist to steady me, and his own laughter came warm and ticklish against my hair.

I looked up. His face was near mine, his auburn curls damp at his temples and his eyes sparkling. And his lips—gulp—his lips were a hairbreadth away from mine.

I was acutely aware of the blush burning my cheeks, my heart battering against my ribs.

The oven timer beeping made us startle and draw apart, and then neither one of us knew where to look. To avoid the awkwardness, I focused on sliding my cookies from the oven. Flynn did the same.

I examined my cookies with a critical eye but found that I was happy with the way they'd plumped in the oven. They were crisp on the outside with gooey, Amul-chocolate-stuffed centers. At last, I risked a glance at Flynn and discovered he was holding one of his own golden-brown cookies, a pleased expression on his face.

"Ready to taste-test?" he asked.

I nodded. Slowly, I bit into my warm cookie. The richness of the melted chocolate center was amplified by the surprising but welcome spiciness of the garam masala. The spice blend of nutmeg, cinnamon, and cardamom complemented the chocolate perfectly. The moment I tasted it, I knew. This was the ONE.

"You did it, didn't you?" Flynn grinned at me.

"You tell me." I passed a cookie toward him, and he gave me one of his.

I bit into Flynn's cookie, and it was amazing, like I'd known it would be. He'd created a shortbread-style cookie with a lemon pudding center. There was something else, too—a subtle flavor that gave the lemon an extra zing. I tilted my head, concentrating on deciphering the mystery flavor. "Crushed lavender?"

He nodded appreciatively. "Your sixth sense. At it again."

"It's light and fresh, and tastes like summertime. Now . . . what about mine?"

My pulse ratcheted up as I waited for his verdict. He chewed slowly and met my eyes, nodding in genuine appreciation. "You don't need me to tell you that you did it. You know."

"Yay! Thank you, Flynn." I clapped my hands, then scooped up my phone, my fingers flying over the screen. "I'm going to submit the recipe to Cookie Crumbles right now, while everything is still fresh in my—"

My words were cut off by my cell phone's ring. My heart sank as our home number scrolled across the screen. I glanced at the time. Omigod—it was after eleven! How had it gotten so late?

"Dad?" I said into the phone before my dad even had a chance to speak. "I'm sorry, I lost track of time." I heard Dad's sharp intake of breath and guessed he was about to launch into a lecture. I preempted him with a lightning-quick "Be home in a few. Loveyoubye."

I didn't even have to explain to Flynn that I needed to go. He was already handing me my bag as I pocketed my phone.

"I'll walk you home," he offered, and only a few minutes later, the shop was locked up and we were strolling past the harbor. Waves lapped quietly against the pier's wooden pylons as the lights from the docked boats winked on the water.

"So what's your verdict on sailing?" I asked him.

"Fun," he answered. "But too . . ."

"Wet?" I offered.

He laughed. "Too overwhelming to do alone, I think."

"Okay. I get that. What should we try next? Kayaking? Tae kwon do? Ballroom dancing?"

"No dancing." He smiled. "The mop would be too jealous."

I laughed, and warmth cascaded through me at the memory of our dance. We left the harbor behind and, after another block, turned onto my street.

"Well . . . we're not stopping until you find your heartsease, remember?" I told Flynn.

"You don't give up, do you?" I shook my head, and his smile widened as we reached the front steps of my house. "I don't know when I'll have the time for more experimentation."

"We made time today and we'll do it again. No problem." I faced him in the porch light's golden glow, butterflies taking flight inside me as I noticed how the dim light made the contours of his angular face more prominent and—gulp—even cuter.

His expression was thoughtful. "You're serious. You'd spend more of your spare time trying to find me a hobby? Even after

I've been so obnoxious to you? When you barely have a second to yourself with the twins as it is?"

I shrugged. "Sure. It's what I'd do for anyone I care about." The words were out of my mouth before I realized their weight, and then I couldn't bring myself to look at him for fear of what I might see in his expression. "I should, um, get inside." I quickly turned toward the door.

"Mina, wait." Flynn caught my hand in his, and my breath froze in my throat. He dropped my hand in a millisecond, glancing down awkwardly. "I—"

"See you tomorrow!" I blurted, hoping I'd get in the door before I melted from mortification. Then I tried to erase the awkwardness by adding a joking "But you better eat some humble pie before bed, because my cookies are going to outsell your cookies, and I'll be the reigning cookie champ!"

He laughed. "Dream on!"

I went inside and shut the door, my heart racing. What would he have said if I'd let him? Would he have said he felt like we were becoming friends? Or—maybe *more* than friends? Was that even possible when we'd gotten off to such a rocky start? I smiled into the darkness, pressing my fingers to the spot where his hand had touched mine. What was happening? I hardly knew.

But even my dad's lecture about my lateness couldn't put a damper on my mood. Up in my room, as the clock struck midnight, I hit submit on my recipe entry for the Cookie Crumbles contest. A few minutes later, I lay in bed knowing that sleep would be a long time coming but not caring. I had the perfect recipe, and the perfect solution to my family's problems. More than that, the memory of dancing with Flynn kept me smiling as my eyes drifted closed at last.

Chapter Eight

On the way to school the next morning, I stopped into A Batch Made in Heaven and learned that the shop had already sold out of my I Like You Choco-lot Garam Masala Cookies. Which made me the champion of my Battle of the Bakers competition with Flynn.

"Gloat much?" Flynn teased when I performed a victory dance in the shop's dining room. But he didn't seem at all surprised (or upset) that my cookies were instant hits.

As the two of us walked to school together, I told Flynn that

I wanted to take him on another "exploratory" excursion that afternoon. He barely even hesitated before agreeing.

"My dad won't be thrilled," he said, "but I'll talk to Hughie and Stella. They'll cover for me."

I had a mental checklist of the places I wanted to take him to. We'd go for a walk along the shoreline on Chuckanut Trail and finish at Oyster Cove Shellfish Farms, my fave spot for local oysters and clams. It was the perfect way to show Flynn the Oyster Cove I knew and loved that he'd never had time to explore.

When we got to school, we went our separate ways—Flynn to the eighth-grade lockers and I to the seventh-grade ones. I felt my phone buzz in my pocket, and when I looked at the screen, I discovered a bunch of texts and three missed calls from Kalli.

The second I saw her name, I knew what I'd done. I reached the library thirty seconds later, out of breath from my sprint across the length of the school. My heart sank as I scoured the tables to find them all empty. Kalli wasn't anywhere to be seen.

Wracked with guilt, I searched the hallways for Kalli and at last spotted her at Jane's locker talking with Jane and Fabs. I called her name, and all three of my friends turned to face me with confused and disappointed looks. My stomach lurched.

I opened my mouth, but Kalli spoke before I could. "You forgot." Her tone was matter-of-fact, but her eyes betrayed her hurt. "I waited in the library for half an hour."

"I'm so sorry!" I blurted. "I stopped by A Batch Made in Heaven, and . . ." I didn't even understand how I could've forgotten, except that thinking about Flynn had suddenly, confusedly, become a habit I was slipping into more and more. "I submitted my recipe for the Cookie Crumbles contest, and I was so excited. I didn't have my head on straight."

Kalli's expression deflated. "You didn't tell me." Her voice was quiet. "About submitting your recipe."

"It happened so fast. I only came up with it last night." I felt another prickle of guilt. For the first time since I could remember, my BFF hadn't been the first person I'd shared my big news with. "I planned to tell you today—"

"But you told Flynn first?" Kalli guessed. She eyed me quizzically. "What's really going on with you two? I mean, we all know how cute he is, but you said you couldn't stand working with him."

"That was in the beginning. It's different now. And he *is* nice."

Kalli's eyes widened. "So you *are* crushing on him."

A hot rush of blood swamped my cheeks. "Noooooooo."

Kalli folded her arms, staring at me expectantly, as if waiting for it to sink into my own brain. My brain, though, wasn't cooperating and could only reel. *Was* I crushing on Flynn? *Maybe*, came my brain's muddled response. But I wasn't ready to say it aloud. Not when I could barely process the idea.

I shook my head, dazed and overwhelmed.

"Fine," Kalli said flatly. "Don't talk to me about it. Whatever."

"Kalli, it's complicated." I sighed. "Look, let's focus on getting you through your presentation. We can practice at lunch. I'll make this right."

"Stop!" The word came out of Kalli's mouth so loudly that I jumped a little. "I'm ready for the presentation. I figured it out. I don't need you to fix me. I can handle it."

"I—I'm not trying to fix you—"

"You always try to solve everybody's problems. It's what you do. But I'm the one giving the presentation. I'm the one who has to deal with my stage fright. You can't solve this, okay?" She shook her head, blowing out a breath. "Everything's fine. *I'm* fine. First period's about to start, and I've got to swing by my locker. See you in a few."

She turned away while Jane and Fabs exchanged uncertain glances. I stared after Kalli with a sinking heart.

Fabs squeezed my arm. "She'll be okay."

"I think she misses you," Jane offered.

"But I'm right here," I responded. Still, when I glanced at Jane and Fabs, I saw doubt on their faces. "Have I really been that distracted lately?"

They nodded simultaneously.

I let out a sigh. "I'll do better."

Still, I couldn't shake the strange unease that I'd felt between me and Kalli. And I didn't know how to make it disappear.

I stared at my inbox on my phone's screen as it refreshed, my stomach tight with anticipation. *Let it be there* was my silent refrain as Tuesday's new emails appeared. But there was nothing from Cookie Crumbles. Nothing since I'd sent the recipe last Wednesday. Nothing for almost a week.

"Earth to Mina." Flynn's voice made me startle, and I nearly dropped my phone into the cup of paint-muddied water.

"Sorry!" I clutched the phone tight. "I'm a little preoccupied."

"I can tell." He smiled and motioned toward my work in progress—the lotus flower I was painting on a serving platter. My plan was to give the platter to my dad for the grand opening of our new restaurant.

I'd decided to take Flynn to Time to Kiln, the paint-your-own-pottery shop in town. But it was rapidly becoming clear that neither of us was feeling the painting vibe today. "You haven't made a single brushstroke for the last five minutes," he told me.

I inspected *his* work in progress—a ceramic cookie jar. He was halfway through painting the words *Bliss in Every Bite* around the jar's lid. The writing looked good, but I had no idea what the blue splotches were supposed to be. "Yours is nice. I like the blue . . . dragons?" I guessed.

Flynn grimaced. "Wings! They're supposed to be the wings on the Batch Made in Heaven logo."

I tilted my head, looking at the splotches from another angle. "Okay, I see it now . . ."

"You're a horrible liar." He broke into laughter, tossing his brush onto the table. "It's obvious that painting is not going to be my 'thing.'"

"Mine, either." I laughed, too, relieved that I could drop the pretense of being focused on painting. "I'd so much rather be baking. And? I think I'm way too distracted today."

"No word from Cookie Crumbles yet?" Flynn asked, reading my mind.

I shook my head. Waiting was beginning to feel like torture. I couldn't focus at school, and I'd flubbed a math quiz that should've been easy for me. My parents had asked me more than once if I was feeling all right. All I could do was nod, when truly I felt like a rubber band pulled too taut. I gave Flynn a glum glance. "The guidelines said that finalists would be notified within a week of the submission deadline."

"And you think the silence means you've lost the contest." He studied me with those piercing eyes that, lately, seemed so adept at unpuzzling my every mood.

"Maybe," I conceded, grateful that I could share my doubts with him.

"And I'll bet that Kalli already scolded you for that defeatist attitude, so I'm not going to touch that minefield." He held up his hands, backing away from me.

I smiled, then sobered. "Actually . . . I haven't talked much to Kalli about it." That was an understatement. I hadn't talked to her about it at all. More often than not, Fabs or Jane had to nudge me during lunch to get me to snap back to whatever conversation they were having. And Kalli . . . Kalli seemed distant. Not angry, but not herself, either. She'd stopped telling me about the museum or asking me about my afternoons at the shop. And she hadn't mentioned Flynn at all since last week. The easy candor we'd always had was suddenly wound tight with tension, and we'd shifted into a politeness that was more fitting for acquaintances than BFFs. But her docent presentation was later today, in a little over an hour, and I hoped that we'd have a chance to clear the air then. Only, I wasn't sure what I could say *to* clear the air.

I realized that Flynn was studying my expression, concern on his face.

He offered me an understanding smile. "Hey, no matter what happens, you invented an amazing cookie recipe. And you don't need some contest to prove what a great baker you are."

"Thanks," I said softly. "But that's not enough."

"Because then you won't be able to help make your parents' restaurant happen?" he asked. When I nodded, he added carefully, "I'm not sure you have as much control over that as you think you do."

"What do you mean?" My stomach knotted.

"You think winning is going to change everything, but you told me your dad is dragging his feet about calling Mrs. Yang," Flynn said. "I know from when my dad was a chef what a huge time commitment a restaurant is. Maybe your dad's having second thoughts."

"No way." I stiffened. "He's wanted to do this for years!"

"Okay, okay!" Flynn said. "I don't know him, and you do."

"That's right. And the restaurant's going to work." My voice was firm even as my pulse wavered. Dad wouldn't have second thoughts, would he?

"Hey." Flynn leaned closer, and for a second our foreheads were nearly touching. "I didn't mean to upset you. *I* think you're a shoo-in to win, as talented as you are."

I smiled as some of the tension in my shoulders released. "Talented enough to outbake you," I said teasingly.

"Ouch." Flynn clutched his chest like I'd launched an arrow at his heart, which only made me laugh harder and swat him with the corner of my painting smock. Then I shrieked as he lunged for me.

"Take that back," he said as he tickled me.

"Never," I wheezed between hiccuping laughs.

"You've given me no choice," he said then, and smeared a dollop of paint across my cheek.

I gasped in surprise. "Oh . . . this means war." I scooped up a fingerful of paint and splatted it onto his cheek.

He burst out laughing as he reached for more paint, and I armed myself with a brush. Wielding it like a sword, I jabbed and parried around our paint station as Flynn landed a few splats on my cheeks and nose.

As I ducked under his arm, he grabbed me around the waist and spun me to face him. I lost my breath as I glanced at the cupid's bow in his upper lip, spellbound by its curve, so well-defined and—gulp—adorably kissable.

"Excuse me. What exactly is going on here?"

Instantly, Flynn and I leapt apart. Mrs. Pattersby, the shop's owner, was standing nearby, taking in our paint-smeared faces.

Heat pricked my cheeks, but Flynn let out a chuckle, which made me snort-giggle into my hand.

"Just having a little fun," he said. "We'll clean up. Don't worry."

Ten minutes and one big cleaning spree later, we were walking down Main Street, still cracking up over our painting debacle. But when Flynn's phone rang, the moment he answered it, his smile dimmed.

"I know, Dad," he said, "but Hughie told me it was fine. He and Stella had everything taken care of—"

I couldn't hear what Mr. Winston was saying, but the frustration flashing quick as a thunderbolt across Flynn's face told me it wasn't good. At last, with the phone gripped tightly in his hand, Flynn said in a harsh tone, "Well, maybe you should start inventing the recipes, then."

With that, he hit end on the screen and shoved the phone into his pocket.

I stared at Flynn, not quite believing what I'd heard. "Did you just tell your dad off?" I whispered.

"He was on my case about not coming into the shop after school. Even though I told him this morning what the plan was." Flynn scowled. "I'm so tired of this game of pretend. And of feeling guilty every second I'm not at the shop."

"Maybe your dad doesn't realize how you feel." I laid a hand gently on his arm. "Have you tried talking to him about it?"

Flynn shook his head. "I wanted to wait until I really had a reason to. I guess our time together trying new things kind of inspired me." He sucked in a breath. "I'm meeting Trent and Will at the archery range during lunch tomorrow. I want to try some shooting. They've been asking to teach me for months, but I always said no. I figured I'd never have time to join the team. But it's something I've wanted for a while. I've just never allowed myself to think about it as a real possibility."

"That's great!" I said.

"We'll see." But his voice was so full of hope, it was obvious how much he wanted it to work. "Hey, do you want to come along? We could try it together. It might help take your mind off the contest for a little while?"

My answer came without a moment's hesitation. "I'd love that." I had the urge to reach for his hand, to feel his fingers intertwined with mine. My pulse drummed as realization flooded through me. My keen awareness of every move Flynn made, of every shift in his expression. The thrill I felt whenever he was near. They were all clues pointing to one fact, and suddenly, I was sure what it was.

I actually gasped, and Flynn turned around. "Mina?" He stepped toward me, looking concerned. "Are you okay?"

"I'm fine," I said, nearly laughing with giddiness. "I—I have to go!" I was rambling, and my cheeks were on fire. But I didn't want him guessing the reason why. Not yet. My discovery was too new, and there was someone else I needed to talk to first. "Kallie's presentation starts in ten minutes. I've got to get over to the museum."

"Oh . . . right." Flynn nodded, but his expression was confounded. "Okay. So, um, meet me at the range during lunch tomorrow."

"Great!" I chirped. "See you then."

With a smile and a trilling heart, I jogged to the museum.

Chapter Nine

"Chinook tribal members of the Pacific Northwest still honor the traditions of our ancestors," Kalli said, her eyes scanning the audience with poise and confidence that didn't betray even a hint of nervousness. "We hope to keep the stories and history of our people alive and thriving. Thank you."

The audience gathered around the exhibit at the museum burst into enthusiastic applause. Kalli smiled in thanks. When I whistled through my teeth, I was glad to see her giggle. I felt as if I'd broken through one of the barriers that had been raised between us over the past few days.

The museum's special living history presentation about the Native American tribes of Washington State had drawn a crowd of about thirty, which was pretty impressive, considering the size of our small town. Kalli's grandparents, parents, and brothers had all been in the audience, beaming proudly as Kalli spoke about her heritage. Now I watched as a reporter for the local *Oyster Cove Times* approached Kalli, asking for an interview. The reporter looked familiar to me, even though I couldn't think where I might've seen him before.

Probably just around town, I figured.

I walked through the exhibits, admiring the artwork and artifacts, while Kalli finished up her interview. I waited until she'd greeted her family with hugs. Then I rushed toward her with my arms outstretched and grabbed her in a congratulatory hug, too.

"Can you spare a few minutes for a plebian, or are you too famous for that now?" I asked teasingly.

Kalli laughed, then breathed out a sigh of relief. "Thank goodness that's over. My knees were shaking the entire time!"

"You were amazing! And you didn't look nervous at all!"

She smiled. "It was actually fun, when I wasn't worried about forgetting everything I was saying. And the reporter from the *Oyster Cove Times* who's doing a piece on the town's mentorship program said I'd be one of the featured students, so that's exciting. He asked me a bunch of questions about the program." She nudged my shoulder. "I mentioned you, too."

"Really?" I asked in surprise.

She nodded. "Of course. I had to brag about how my BFF is busy baking the world's best cookies at A Batch Made in Heaven, and how she's going to be as famous as Bakerella someday."

I looked at her, suddenly seeing anew how considerate Kalli was, and how she'd always supported and encouraged me. It was one of the reasons why we were such great friends, but somehow, in the last couple of weeks, I'd nearly forgotten that. "Thank you, Kalli," I said softly, then cleared my throat. "Actually . . . I owe you an apology. I know I've been acting a little strange lately and keeping you at arm's length."

"Yeah," she said quietly. "And . . . you sort of downplayed what a big deal this was for me."

My mouth dropped open, and I stared at her. "What? How?"

"When I told you how nervous I was, you just kept telling me not to worry. That it would all be fine. Acting like you could actually make my nervousness go away." She locked eyes with me. "You always act like you can fix everything, even when you can't." She sighed. "I just needed you to listen. To be there for me. *Not* to solve the problem for me."

"Omigod." I sank onto a bench in the museum's lobby. Kalli sat down beside me. "I had no idea that's how I came across. I didn't mean to make you feel that way. I just wanted to make you feel better."

She smiled. "I know. And I've been wanting to talk to you about this for a long time, but you've been so busy."

"I got caught up in inventing recipes for the contest and . . ." I shrugged. "You know how I can get sometimes."

She nodded. "Tunnel vision," we said at the same time, and then laughed.

"You've been spending so much time with Flynn," she conceded, "but whenever I asked you about it, you . . ."

"Got defensive." I blushed. "Things were getting . . . complicated. I'm not even sure I realized what was happening until today."

"When you realized that you're crushing on Flynn for real?" Kalli asked, in a confident tone that said she already knew the answer to that question.

I nodded, a ridiculously goofy smile spreading across my face. My heart had been teetering on a high wire in my chest, and now I knew, beyond a doubt, that it was falling. "I can't stop thinking about him," I admitted.

"I *knew* it!" Kalli cried victoriously. "That day when I saw you and Flynn at the dock. I could totally tell from the look on your face that you were a goner. But . . . I wanted *you* to tell *me*." She grinned and nudged my side. "Do you think he likes you, too?"

I thought about how Flynn had changed in the past few weeks, and the fun we'd been having together. "Maybe? He seems to like spending time with me, but—"

"You should tell him." Kalli gave me a knowing look. "Make

the first move. I could never do that, but you're so much braver than me."

"Not about this stuff," I said. Just the thought made my heart gallop. "Besides, you're a lot bolder than you give yourself credit for," I told my bestie, and she smiled.

An idea occurred to me, and I sat up straight. "I'm meeting Flynn at the archery range during lunch period tomorrow. Maybe I could talk to him then." *If* I was brave enough.

"You, Flynn, and bows and arrows?" Kalli giggled. "All you need is Cupid and a shot through the heart." She stood up, hands to her chest, and started crooning the old Bon Jovi song "Shot Through the Heart." Within seconds, I was bent over laughing so hard a little snort snuck out, which only made me laugh harder. Kalli collapsed into laughter, too, and suddenly, I was overcome with gratitude. Only Kalli could ever make me laugh this hard. It felt so good to be like this again with her, the recent awkwardness erased.

Kalli's entire family came over to join us then. Kalli's parents invited me to their house for a big celebratory dinner. After texting my parents to get their okay, I happily accepted.

Within minutes, Kalli and I were trailing her family down Main Street, arm in arm and talking easily, just like we had since we were little.

The next day, I watched as Flynn drew the arrow back, holding the position for a long, breathless moment. His expression was intense with concentration, his eyes energized, his jawline flexing in a way that made it hard for me to look anywhere else. Seeing him try archery for the first time was a heady, pulse-pounding experience that I didn't want to end. He was so intent with his focus that I could stare unabashedly, without a chance of him noticing.

Earlier that lunch period, when Flynn had left the cafeteria to head to the range, Kalli had practically yanked me from my seat. "Go! Go! Hurry!" she'd said urgently.

"*Never* chase boys," I'd said to her. It was a motto we'd often repeated to each other. "We're too strong for that."

But the fact was, my heart felt like a rabbit springing from hope to hope. *Did* Flynn like me as much as I liked him? Would I have the courage to let him know how I felt about him?

Now I watched as Flynn released the arrow with a soft, whispering *whoosh*. It flew straight and sure across the room and landed with a decisive *thwack* at the edge of the target.

"Impressive for your first try," Trent said. "Most everybody would've missed the target completely."

Flynn lowered the recurve bow and glanced toward me, grinning.

"You know, it's not charming to look so pleased with yourself," I teased.

He raised an eyebrow, his grin widening. "Aha! You think I'm charming when I'm *not* looking so pleased with myself?"

"Wha— Oh! That's not what I . . ." I laughed, my cheeks burning, then tried to downplay my embarrassment with a cool "Smart aleck."

He laughed, shaking his curls off his forehead, but there seemed to be a new light in his eyes, as if he found my discomfiture appealing, and even hoped for. "Come on." He held the bow out to me. "Your turn."

"The draw weight is set at forty pounds," Trent told me as Flynn handed me the bow. "You might have a tough time drawing the bow."

"Huh." I smiled craftily, keeping to myself the knowledge that I regularly carried both of the fifteen-pound twins without any trouble at all. "I hope I can manage" was all I said.

I'd been paying close attention when Trent had shown Flynn how to hold the bow, and now I mirrored the same motions, smoothly drawing the string back. "Like this?" I glanced at Flynn and Trent, and stifled a giggle when I caught the look of surprise on Flynn's face.

"Whoa," he said. "Remind me never to challenge you to an arm-wrestling contest."

I laughed as I took aim, trying to replicate the way I'd seen both Trent and Flynn line the arrow up with the bow site. But knowing that Flynn was watching broke my concentration.

When I released the arrow, it flew wildly and wobbling, missing the target and striking the door. I was even more mortified to discover that the arrow's tip had lodged itself in the door.

"Oops." I was relieved to see half a dozen other holes in the wood paneling. Clearly, I wasn't the only one who'd shot wild. "How about best two out of three?" I said to Flynn.

"You're on," Flynn replied.

We grinned at each other until Trent cleared his throat. I noticed Trent looking back and forth between Flynn and me, a mischievous smile on his face. "Okay . . . why don't you guys keep practicing while Will and I get some more arrows from the rec room? We're going to need extras."

Trent and Will were elbowing each other and whispering as they walked out of the room, and I had the distinct impression they were leaving on purpose to give Flynn and me some time alone together.

I didn't dare look at Flynn as I fit an arrow back into the bow's notch and faced the target again.

"Hang on," Flynn said. He placed his hands on my waist, and

my pulse danced in my throat. "I think you might need to turn a little bit more . . . like that." The feel of his soft breath at the base of my neck made my own breath disappear. I wanted to stay like this forever, to sink back into his arms, to forget all about the bow and arrow. He whispered, "Let it fly."

I released the arrow and my breath simultaneously, and this time the arrow flew straight, hitting the outer edge of the target.

"Yes!" I cried victoriously.

Flynn smiled, then raised his own bow. After a moment's focus, he shot, and his arrow landed just left of the bull's-eye.

"Better," he said, more to himself than to me. Then he glanced at me, an expression of sheer delight on his face.

"You like this, don't you?" I guessed.

He nodded. "It feels amazing. I could totally see myself getting into archery. But I'm still glad you didn't get a bull's-eye on your first try."

"Why? You'd find that too intimidating?" I challenged him, cocking an eyebrow.

He shook his head, and a blush began spreading from his ears toward his cheeks. "More like too irresistible," he said quietly.

"Oh," I breathed, not having the words to say anything else. I dropped my gaze, afraid that my eyes would reveal too much happiness. Did he mean "irresistible" in a teasing way or in a serious, I-like-you way? "Um—"

My phone chimed, startling us both. I slid the phone from my back pocket and checked the screen.

"Omigod," I whispered. "It's an email from Cookie Crumbles."

"Finally!" Flynn exclaimed. He smiled at me expectantly, but I froze in fear, my hand hesitating over the email icon. "Come on, Mina! You're killing me with the suspense. What are you waiting for?"

I nodded, steeling myself. "Okay. Here goes." I clicked on the icon, closed my eyes for a second, then opened them to read the email:

Dear Ms. Kapur,

Congratulations on being accepted as one of the finalists for the Cookie Crumbles Inc. Recipe Contest . . .

My whoop of excitement echoed off the walls of the range. "I'm in! I'm a finalist!"

"Yes!" Flynn cried, grinning.

"I can't wait to tell my parents!" I hopped up and down. "My dad is going to be so surprised. This is going to change everything, and he'll open his restaurant, and—and . . ."

Flynn's arms wrapped around me in an exuberant hug. "I knew you'd make it!"

I hugged him back, feeling his warmth. He didn't break our hug, and neither did I. We were on the cusp of the hug going on for too long to be a "just friends" type of congratulations, but . . . what if *he* only intended this as a friendly hug? Was *I* the one holding on for too long?

Reluctantly, I stepped back, both of us skirting the other's gaze.

"Mina." Flynn cleared his throat, his cheeks reddening beneath his freckles. When his eyes met mine, my heart sprinted. He looked like he was about to say something important, and I hoped, oh, I hoped, that it might be something about his feelings for me. "I, um, I think I like—"

The door to the range flew open with a bang that made us jump, and then my name was shrieked as Kalli flew into the room with Fabs and Jane beside her.

"You're one of the finalists!" Kalli cried, and then all three of my friends had surrounded me in a group hug.

"I know!" I cried, but then stopped, looking at them in confusion. "Wait, how did you find out? I literally *just* got the email."

"Fabs and I were in the press room going over some last-minute edits for tomorrow's paper," Jane said. "And a press release from Cookie Crumbles came through announcing that the finalists had been selected, and your name was right there at the top!"

There was another collective shriek, followed by more hugging. I caught Flynn's eyes through the tangle of my friends' embrace. He was smiling, but he also looked slightly disappointed, as if he hadn't wanted our "moment" interrupted. If it had actually been a moment. Maybe it had only been in my imagination.

The bell rang, jolting me from my thoughts. My friends were ushering me out the door, asking a torrent of questions about the contest. I could only shrug laughingly in response, because I hadn't even had a chance to read through all the details in the Cookie Crumbles email.

I glanced back at Flynn, who grinned, raising his hand in goodbye. "I'll see you tomorrow!" he called after me.

Then I was practically being carried down the hallway by the momentum of Kalli's enthusiasm as she announced to everyone passing us in the hallway that her BFF was a famous baker. Even as I relished the moment, part of my heart stayed behind with Flynn, wishing it could know what was in his.

Chapter Ten

After school, I threw open my front door and ran inside my house. "Mom? Dad? Where are you?" I called.

I'd been smiling nonstop since lunchtime and had sat through the last classes of the day without hearing a word of the lessons, doodling cookies in my binder when I should've been taking notes. All I could think about was the contest, and the thrilled look I'd see on my parents' faces when I told them the news.

I dropped my schoolbag in the kitchen and bounded up the stairs. My parents were tiptoeing out of the nursery, easing the door shut behind them. Mom lifted a finger to her lips to motion for me to be quiet, so I waved silently but frantically for them to follow me downstairs where we could talk.

"Of course the twins both had to get colds at the same time," Mom mumbled tiredly as she followed me into the kitchen, kneading her forehead. "They're so stuffy."

"I'll fix us some chai." Dad's voice was weary as he put the kettle on the stove.

Neither of them had even glanced my way yet, but now I planted myself between them. "I have some great news!" I sang out.

Mom gave me an affectionate smile around an enormous yawn, rubbing my cheek with the back of her hand. "Mary Poppins is coming to rescue us all?" she joked.

I shook my head. "A couple of weeks ago, I entered a recipe contest for Cookie Crumbles Inc. And"—I heaved an excited breath—"I found out today that I'm a finalist!"

Dad's eyes lit, and he brought his hands together in a thunderous clap. "Wow! That's wonderful! I didn't know you'd entered a recipe contest."

I grinned. "I wanted to surprise you. I've been working on recipes for weeks."

Dad was still smiling, but he also looked confused. "But . . . where? When?"

"At A Batch Made in Heaven," I explained. "Whenever I had extra time in the afternoons."

Mom frowned. "So that's why you've been staying so long at the shop? Instead of coming right home? It hasn't been for your mentorship?"

"Well . . . yes," I said slowly, confused by Mom's frown. Why didn't she look happier about my news? Was she afraid I'd somehow overstayed my welcome at the shop? "Mom, they said it was fine for me to go into the shop whenever I wanted. Hughie and Stella liked having the extra help." Before my mom could ask more questions, I decided to push ahead with my other fantastic news. When my parents heard the rest of what I had to tell them, they'd be over the moon. "And now I can go to Seattle to be in a bake-off! We get to stay in a hotel for free! And it's all going to be livestreamed for the Cookie Crumbles YouTube channel, and—"

"Seattle?" Mom's frown deepened. "When?"

My pulse had begun to sound a doomsday knell, but I kept talking, convinced that my enthusiasm would eventually spread to them. "The weekend of November fifth. But we have to arrive the Thursday before. On Friday we'll get a tour of the Cookie Crumbles baking plant, and all the finalists get interviewed beforehand . . . " I was rambling now, my words pouring out in a frenzied rush. "Travel expenses are all paid for, and—"

Mom held up her hand. "Mina." She sighed and exchanged a glance with Dad. While Mom looked decidedly unhappy, Dad's expression was more one of reluctant regret. "We can't drop everything to take you to Seattle," Mom said. "I already took the day off today because the babies are sick. It's not easy for me to take more personal days now, right after my return from maternity leave. The twins are too young to be left with a sitter for a whole weekend. Even if I stayed here while your father took you, I wouldn't be able to juggle work and both the babies alone. And taking them with us will be too difficult."

"But I—" I stared at her, unable to believe what I was hearing. "I *have* to do this. I'm a finalist."

Mom shook her head. "You've been dishonest with us. All that extra time you spent at the shop, you told us you were working for Mr. Winston. We thought it was for your mentorship. Not for some . . . some whim!"

"This isn't a whim," I said through clenched teeth. Anger bloomed, dark and thorny, inside me. "And I wasn't lying. I kept it a secret from you so that I could surprise you! Can't you see that?" I threw up my hands. "You don't even know why—"

"We needed you at home to help with your sister and brother," Mom said, "and instead you were chasing after this silliness."

"The contest isn't silly." I fought down a lump in my throat. "You act like baking is a waste of my time. You do that to Dad, too—"

"Mina!" Dad's voice held a note of warning but also surprise.

I held my mother's gaze. "You don't want us to open a

restaurant here. I know you don't!" Mom's eyes widened and her mouth opened, but I hurried to add, "And I *have* been helping with Amul and Banita. I help all the time!"

"Mina, we have to do what's best for our family," Dad said quietly. "There will be other contests. It's not the end of the world if you don't participate in this one."

I stared at him, not believing what I was hearing. "But *this* is the contest I want to participate in!" They weren't listening to a word I said. "If I won, there's a shopping spree, and I—"

"This isn't just about you, Mina," Mom said. "We have the twins to think about, too."

Suddenly, all my frustration of the past few months catapulted from my chest into my throat. "The twins are *all* you think about!" I yelled. My hands balled into fists, my entire body turning rigid. "You stopped thinking about me the second they were born!"

Dad's face grew stern with disappointment and anger. "You don't speak to us this way, Mina—"

"How else do I get you to listen?" I brushed past them both, heading for the stairs, but whirled on my heels to face them one last time. "All I am to you now is some sort of . . . permanent babysitter! I'm so sick of it!"

My words bounced off the kitchen walls as my parents frowned at me. Suddenly, a wail rose from the nursery, and Mom gripped the counter in dismay.

"Now you've done it," she said. "You've woken them up with your yelling. Never did I think I'd hear such words from my own daughter." She jabbed a finger toward the ceiling. "Go to your room. Now. Forget about this contest and the trip to Seattle."

"You can't take it away from me!" I cried.

"Upstairs. Go!" Mom's voice was clipped and impermeable.

My eyes filled with tears, and I glanced at Dad, hoping he'd say something to help. He looked at me from under lowered eyelids. "You heard your mother." His voice was a whisper, leaden with disappointment. "Go."

My tears spilled onto my burning cheeks as I stumbled up the stairs to my bedroom. I slammed the door shut, relishing the long-forgotten sound. I was sick of tiptoeing around the house all the time, walking on eggshells during every one of the twins' naps.

I flopped facedown on my bed, giving in to a sob session that felt long overdue. For the past few months, I'd tried my hardest, and Mom and Dad couldn't even see it! I'd been so sure that they'd be thrilled about the contest. Instead, all they'd done was scold me.

I stifled another sob into my pillow as a soft knock sounded on my bedroom door.

"Mina?" Dad's voice sounded more tired than I'd ever heard it. "Please. Let me in."

"Go away" was my choked response.

I sensed him hesitating on the other side of the door. My heart ached.

Another minute passed, and then I heard his footsteps retreating down the hall. Fresh tears welled in my eyes, and I nearly called him back but stopped myself. If he didn't understand now, he never would.

Instead, I grabbed my cell and dialed Flynn's number. He didn't pick up, and I guessed that the shop was inundated with customers. I tried Kalli next and felt a wave of relief when she picked up.

"Hey there, Cookie Crumbles superstar!" Kalli sang cheerily into the phone, which was all it took for me to break into a fresh bout of crying. "Whoa . . ." Kalli's tone instantly morphed into worry. "What's wrong?"

In halting breaths, I told her about the blowup with my parents, and how they'd forbidden me from going to Seattle.

"They don't mean it." Kalli's voice was tinged with disbelief. "They can't. This is the chance of a lifetime!"

I sighed, wiping my eyes with a sodden tissue. "They'll never change their minds."

"Maybe if you apologized—"

"I didn't do anything wrong!" I cried.

"Okay, okay," Kalli said quietly. "But then . . . what about Seattle?"

I sat bolt upright, inspiration striking. "I'm still going." My voice was resolute.

"But . . . your parents just said—"

"I'll go without them. There are buses that go to Seattle from the Oyster Cove bus terminal." The words were rushing from my mouth, my heart matching their pace. "I'll go and win the contest."

"You can't do that," Kalli whispered, sounding horrified by the idea. "That's like running away. What if something happened to you and no one knew where you were? What if you got lost in Seattle? What if—"

"No. No catastrophic thinking allowed," I said firmly, knowing Kalli would go on like that until she was practically hyperventilating from all her imagined worst-case scenarios. I flipped open my laptop and turned it on. "I'm going. That's it." Kalli stayed silent, and I could practically hear her biting her tongue. "We'll talk more tomorrow. Just . . . don't tell anybody about my plan. Okay?"

There was a long pause, and I held my breath, but finally, Kalli said, "Okay. I promise."

"Thanks."

I hung up and turned my full attention to my computer screen as my emails loaded. I opened the one from Cookie Crumbles. Before I lost my nerve, I filled out the permission slip and release forms for the contest. When I came to the electronic signature line at the bottom of the forms, guilt wrenched my heart. I'd never done anything this deceptive in my entire life. What I was about to do was wrong, but my parents were wrong, too. This was the only way.

Sucking in my breath, I filled in my mom's name on the forms and then emailed them back to Cookie Crumbles. I was going to Seattle for the bake-off, and no one was going to stop me.

Chapter Eleven

I arrived at school the next morning with a headache from lack of sleep. Mom had left for work early that morning and was gone by the time I came downstairs, groggy and grumpy. Dad was consumed with wiping the twins' runny noses and trying, unsuccessfully, to soothe their fussiness. I'd eaten as quickly as possible and only offered a monotone goodbye before hurrying out the door. I couldn't look Dad in the eye.

Now I plodded to my locker, my stomach knotted with guilt. When I glanced up to see Flynn waiting for me, I instantly brightened. But then I noticed his expression and froze. His face was stormy with anger.

"Flynn?" I doubled my pace, closing the gap between us. "What's wrong?"

"This." He held up a copy of the morning's *Oyster Cove Times* and jabbed a finger at the front-page headline. It read:

FAKE IT TILL YOU BAKE IT: BOGUS BAKER UNCOVERED AT A BATCH MADE IN HEAVEN

I read the headline, dizzy with confusion. "I—I don't understand—"

"The article says that *I'm* the one inventing the recipes at the shop." Flynn's voice was clipped and cold. "That *I'm* my dad's best kept secret."

"But . . . how could they know that?" I stammered, my pulse quickening. "Nobody knows except—"

"You." Flynn leveled his gaze at me. "You knew."

My heart slammed into my throat. "Wait . . . you think I told them?"

Flynn scowled. "How else would they have found out?"

Hurt and shock flooded me. "I promised I'd never tell anyone, and I didn't. I swear! Not even Kalli. *No one*, Flynn."

He shook his head. "You knew I was frustrated with the way things were. You were pushing me to talk to my dad. You wanted the truth to come out. What am I supposed to think?"

Anger struck lightning hot in my veins. "You're *supposed* to believe me." I stared at him, my voice rising. "I'd never intentionally hurt you or your dad that way. And the fact that you even *think* that . . ." I turned around, forgetting about the notebooks I needed from my locker. Tears pricked my eyes, and all I could think about was getting to the bathroom before they fell. "I thought you knew me better than that," I managed to choke out over my shoulder.

I rushed down the hall, the first tears scalding my face just as I threw open the bathroom door.

"Here you go." Kalli handed me another wad of toilet paper so that I could wipe my eyes for what felt like the hundredth time. My cheeks were chapped from tears and toilet paper. "I'm definitely putting 'tissues' on the student council to-do list. The bathrooms need a rom-dram supply ASAP."

"This isn't a rom-dram!" The words only made me cry harder. "Flynn *hates* me!"

Kalli squeezed my shoulder. "No. He doesn't. But he was totally wrong to accuse you of leaking his identity to the press." She pulled up the article on her phone, reading out loud. "'The real secret ingredient in the famous cookies at A Batch Made in Heaven is a person. And it's not Cookie King Ed Winston. It has recently been uncovered that Mr. Winston's son, Flynn Winston, is the true genius behind the shop's irresistible recipes—'"

"I don't understand how the press found out!" I wrung the damp toilet paper in my hands. "I was never even around someone from the *Oyster Cove Times*!"

Kalli shook her head, and there was a moment of silence as we both scoured our memories. Suddenly, our eyes locked. "The museum!" we cried in unison.

"Oh no." Kalli gasped, slapping a hand to her mouth. "On the day of my living history presentation, I talked to that reporter from the *Times* . . ."

I nodded. "You mentioned my apprenticeship at A Batch Made in Heaven?" My voice squeaked with nerves, and a queasiness churned in my stomach. "Do you remember if you mentioned Flynn?"

Kalli's face paled, and she reluctantly nodded. "I told the reporter that you were working with Flynn at the shop."

"But you didn't know that he was inventing the recipes. How—" I gasped as a memory sledgehammered my brain. "Omigod! I knew I'd seen that reporter somewhere before. The night that I invented my recipe for Cookie Crumbles, he came into the shop after closing. He said he wanted to buy cookies, but Flynn had left his recipe book open on the counter." I covered my face with my hands. "I hid the book right away, but maybe the reporter had seen it before we realized he was in the shop. Maybe he even took a photo of it with his phone? All he would've needed to do was compare the handwriting in the book with another sample. Flynn takes down orders by hand at the shop . . ." I groaned. "It wouldn't have been that hard to figure out."

"Sounds possible," Kalli conceded.

I nodded forlornly, my shoulders drooping. "Now what?"

Kalli brightened. "Tell Flynn your theory about what happened. And then you can make up." She smiled dreamily. "And you get your first kiss, and—"

I scoffed. "Kiss? Are you kidding? He accused me of breaking his trust! He completely insulted me! Why should I explain anything to him?"

Kalli put a hand on my arm. "But, Mina, you *like* him—"

"*He's* in the wrong. Unless he realizes it, I'm over him as of *right now*." I crossed my arms stubbornly, glaring at Kalli to prove my point.

She opened her mouth, probably to try to convince me otherwise, but the bell rang. She shouldered her bag and hugged me, giving me a worried glance. "We've got to go. Think you can handle first period?"

I heaved one last sniffle and nodded. Then another horrible

realization struck me. "Oh no. I told Hughie that I'd help out at Batch after school today. Just to get them through the afternoon rush."

Kalli grimaced. "Ouch. Well, it's not your mentorship day. You don't have to . . ."

"I have to at least stop by for a little bit. I can't leave them hanging." I sighed, dreading the idea of setting foot in the shop after what had just happened. There was no bandage big enough to repair this type of hurt.

My steps were leaden as I made my way to A Batch Made in Heaven that afternoon. Kalli, Fabs, and Jane had offered me a fortifying group hug before I'd left school. Even though it was comforting to know I had my friends' support, it had done nothing to still my Tilt-A-Whirling stomach. If Flynn had told Mr. Winston about what he believed I'd done, I'd be fired from my mentorship on the spot.

I had no idea what I'd be walking into, but what I definitely didn't expect was the sight that met me when I turned the corner to the shop. I jerked to a stop on the sidewalk, nearly colliding with the long line of customers standing impatiently outside the shop's door. The CLOSED sign was in the window. What was going on?

All around me, customers were whispering and muttering. I picked up on a few people's mentions of the *Times* article. Mostly, though, customers were bummed about not being able to get their favorite cookies. My spirits lifted a bit. What I was hearing wasn't anger at Mr. Winston for the deception. It was only disappointment because customers couldn't enjoy the cookies they loved.

Weaving my way through the crowd, I skirted around the building to the shop's back door, the one that led directly into the Cookie Vault. I knocked persistently, going with my hunch that Mr. Winston was inside. When no one answered, I knocked again, then spoke to the closed door.

"Mr. Winston? Hughie? If you're in there, it's me. Mina. Please. Open the door?"

The door eased open a crack.

"Mina?" Hughie's voice was tentative, but when he saw that it was me, and that I was alone, he quickly ushered me inside. "Thank goodness you're here!" He pressed his hand to his forehead. "I don't know what to do. That article this morning in the *Oyster Cove Times* . . ." He glanced over his shoulder. "Mr. Winston is fuming! He's saying his reputation is ruined and we'll have to close our doors forever!"

"I don't think that's true," I protested.

Just then, Mr. Winston appeared behind Hughie, frowning. *Oh no.* I expected that at any moment Mr. Winston would start yelling at me for exposing his secret. Seconds passed, though, and he didn't. "I should've known it would all catch up to me," he said at last. "Serves me right for hiding behind my son's genius all these years."

"But, Mr. Winston," I said, "I was just out front, and I didn't hear customers complaining about the article. I'm not even sure that they care. At least, not very much."

"I still don't understand how this could've happened," Mr. Winston said. "We've always been so careful."

"So . . . you don't know how the newspaper found out the truth?" I asked carefully.

"No idea," he said.

Relief broke over me. Flynn hadn't thrown me under the bus. At least, not yet. Anger pricked me anew as I thought about his harsh accusation this morning. A voice inside me told me to go home and forget about A Batch Made in Heaven forever. After all, why should I care what happened to the shop after the way Flynn had treated me? Let *him* deal with this problem.

"Where's Flynn?" I asked Hughie and Mr. Winston.

Hughie's face paled. "We don't know! He didn't come to the shop after school the way he always does. He didn't bake a new Cookie of the Day recipe this morning like he usually does, either. He's not answering his cell, and customers started coming. Stella's called out sick. And we don't have a Cookie of the Day."

Hmm. Maybe Flynn had finally had enough of the ruse, but his timing was terrible. "I'm sorry," I began haltingly, "but I can't—"

Help was what I'd been about to say. *I can't help.* But the final word wouldn't form on my lips. As I peered at Hughie's desperate face and Mr. Winston's pained one, I knew that I couldn't abandon them. Flynn had wronged me, yes. And Mr. Winston had been wrong to keep a lie going. But the shop didn't deserve to fall apart. I couldn't let that happen. Not when it was part of my community. Not when I'd come to love working here.

"Okay." My voice took on a determined tone. I reached for one of the aprons hanging on the wall. "Let's see what we can do."

Mr. Winston frowned. "There's nothing we can do. If I open the doors, people will demand answers. What am I going to tell them?"

"Don't tell them anything yet," I responded. "Customers love the cookies and will always love the cookies, no matter *who* is inventing the recipes. And, Mr. Winston, today *you* are going to invent the Cookie of the Day recipe, just like people have always believed you did." I reached for the measuring cups and chocolate chips and then smiled at Mr. Winston's skeptical expression. "Don't worry," I said confidently. "We'll do it together."

*　　*　　*

Three hours later, Mr. Winston nodded a final farewell to the last customer as the woman walked out the door, happily munching a Fabulous Fudge cookie.

"Be sure to come back tomorrow to try the Cookie of the Day!" Hughie called after her.

I let out a sigh of relief as I locked the door and flipped the shop's sign to CLOSED. Every trace of Hughie's panic had vanished, and even Mr. Winston was calm. Layers of flour dusted his chef's coat, and there was a smear of dried cookie dough across his chin, but he looked strangely content.

"*That* was a trial by fire." Hughie blew a wayward lock of his hair off his forehead.

"It wasn't that bad. There was only one *small* fire." I pulled the charred oven mitt from the pocket of my apron. Mr. Winston had ignited the mitt when he'd accidentally touched it to the oven broiler. I grinned at them, and we all laughed.

Mr. Winston bit into a leftover Cookie of the Day. "I put in too much baking soda and not enough vanilla," he pronounced with a critical air. "And I should've added some walnuts." He glanced at me. "I suppose you're going to say I have my work cut out for me?"

"Every great baker does," I replied. "No matter who they are." I grabbed the broom and dustpan from the cleaning closet and began sweeping crumbs from behind the sales counter. I was tired, but it was the rewarding kind of tired—the kind that comes from hours of productivity doing something you love.

At first, Mr. Winston had been unsure, hesitating over mixing flavors and ingredients. "Cookies are nothing like beef bourguignonne," he'd complained. "Why is it so much easier for me to create a perfect dinner than to create an original cookie?"

Even when he launched a mixing bowl across the kitchen in frustration, I stood firm. "Don't give up" was all I kept saying.

While Hughie managed the sales counter and sold what was left of yesterday's cookie stock, I helped Mr. Winston as he tried his hand at recipes. He was exacting when it came to texture and taste, and I was glad to be able to offer him pointers about getting the proportions of the ingredients just right.

Mr. Winston's first trial batch had been overdone and brittle, the second batch too flat. But his third batch showed promise. The best part of it all was that when customers saw him walking through the Cookie Vault door with fresh cookies, they were seeing the Mr. Winston they'd always believed in—the one who invented his own, original recipes.

Now I looked at Mr. Winston, a question on the tip of my tongue that I was afraid to ask. Finally, I mustered the courage. "Are you going to keep inventing your own recipes?"

"I don't know." He thought this over. "It may be time to take a step back and figure out what's right for the shop. But more importantly, what's right for Flynn. I'm probably going to lose some customers because of that article, but maybe that's not the end of the world." He rubbed his forehead. "I've been living a lie for a long time. Flynn has such a natural talent for baking. And he used to love it so much. But I don't know if he does anymore."

I was still upset with Flynn, but I knew how much it might help him to talk with his dad honestly, about everything. "You should talk to Flynn," I said. My voice was tight, my throat stinging with the memory of Flynn's earlier accusations. Despite my lingering anger, I wanted to do this much for him.

Mr. Winston nodded thoughtfully. "I suppose it's time I did. He finally texted me that he'd be here soon."

"I should get home," I said, not wanting to be in the shop when Flynn showed up. "Are you and Hughie okay to finish closing up?"

"Of course! And, Mina?" Mr. Winston cleared his throat. "Thank you."

I smiled and handed him the charred oven mitt. He chuckled as he took it, shaking his head mirthfully. "I may give this a place of honor on the kitchen wall. To commemorate the first day I made one of my *own* famous cookie recipes."

I laughed. "The first day, but hopefully not the last."

I grabbed my bag and hoodie, and stepped out the door into

the chilly autumn air. Mist had rolled in from the Sound, and a light drizzle was falling. I slipped my hood over my head and turned for home. I might not have been able to fix *all* that was wrong today, but helping Mr. Winston had been right, and knowing that, at least, offered a little comfort.

Chapter Twelve

As I walked up the steps to our house, I expected to be met with the same old routine. Dad would have the harried look of a person who'd just endured hours of diaper changes, spit-up, and crying babies. Mom would still be at work, and I'd no doubt find a list of chores I needed to do on the kitchen counter. I bolstered myself as I put my hand on the doorknob, vowing that I'd get my chores done quickly and then retreat to my room without a word to my parents.

When I opened the door, though, my jaw nearly hit the ground. Dad was in the kitchen with Mom, the two of them standing shoulder to shoulder chopping vegetables. Dad was humming along with the music softly playing from his phone, smiling at Mom, more relaxed than I'd seen him in months.

"Mina!" he called quietly but cheerfully. "Come here, beti!"

Tentatively, I drew nearer, feeling as if I'd accidentally stumbled into a parallel universe. "Um . . . what are you doing?" My voice betrayed my shock.

Mom and Dad exchanged a glance, and then Mom looked at me, her eyes glinting with a hint of mischief. "I took the afternoon off and came home early. I've—*we've*—been juggling so much lately. It was time for a breather." She nudged Dad's shoulder, and I wondered if it was meant as some sort of silent signal. "I'm going to peek in on the babies and lie down for a few minutes. Call me when dinner's ready?"

Dad nodded, and Mom paused to plant a soft kiss on my forehead. "No chores today," she said with a mysterious smile. "We all deserve the night off."

I smiled back, surprised and relieved. Then Dad motioned me over to the counter and tossed me my apron. My breath hitched in my throat when I saw the worn book lying beside the cutting board on the counter. It was *Mina and Dad's Recipes.*

"It's time we add a new recipe to our book, don't you think?" The gruff emotion in Dad's voice tugged at my heart, and my eyes inadvertently filled.

I didn't trust myself to say anything without crying, so I nodded, smiled, and slipped on the apron. I admired the array of chopped vegetables on the counter: onions, sweet potato, lotus root, and karela, a bitter gourd that Dad loved to use in curry to add one-of-a-kind flavor. Already, I was envisioning a lamb curry with veggies and the perfect blend of spice and texture.

"How about lamb?" I suggested. "And we can add in some fenugreek leaves, too." My mouth watered at the thought.

"Yes!" Dad nodded enthusiastically. "We'll have a feast, and you'll be our master chef!"

He wasted no time gathering the herbs and spices we needed for the curry sauce, and soon we were working seamlessly side by side, a cozy comfort settling over the kitchen as it filled with the tantalizing aroma of simmering curry. An hour later, as I jotted down the last measurements for the recipe in our book, Mom wandered back into the kitchen, yawning but looking refreshed from her nap.

"Sleep is a wonderful thing," she said. She lifted the lid on the curry pot, breathing in deeply. "That smells amazing."

"It will taste even better," I said as I spooned the thick curry over rice and handed my parents their bowls. "Wait and see."

The three of us sat down, and we all took our first bites. The curry was the perfect blend of savory spices, with a tangy zing of heat at the end of each swallow. The lamb was tender, the flavors of the vegetables and meat fusing into a mouthwatering melody. For a few moments, the only sound was the clinking of our silverware against our bowls, but at last, I risked glances at my parents.

My mom was chewing with her eyes closed, a satisfied smile on her face. "Delicious," she said.

"Menu-worthy," Dad declared.

I beamed at their kind words. "I learned from the best," I told Dad.

He smiled back, but then a wistful expression crossed his face. He glanced at my mom, and they both looked at me.

"Beti, there's something we want to say." Dad took a weighted breath. "We're sorry."

Mom nodded, reaching for my hand. "We've been so consumed with taking care of Amul and Banita. We didn't realize how difficult it must have been for you these last few months."

I swallowed thickly, my throat tightening with emotion. Dad hugged me, tucking me into his burly chest. "We expected too much from you . . ."

"I wanted to make everything better," I said into Dad's shirt. "I love the twins—"

"We know that." Mom began rubbing my back in small circles, something I'd seen her do a hundred times with the babies. I closed my eyes, my breath steadying under the calming effect of her fingertips. "And of course I don't think your baking is silly, *or* a waste of time. I never wanted you to think that . . ." She sighed. "You're not an adult, and we shouldn't have been so hard on you. But you caught us off guard when you told us about the Cookie Crumbles contest—"

"You didn't even listen!" I sat back, wiping my eyes. "I didn't get to tell you why . . ." I gulped. "Why I wanted to enter in the first place!"

Mom gazed at me, softly brushing her hand against my cheek. "So . . . tell us now?"

She and Dad waited while I caught my breath and dried my eyes. "I've loved working at A Batch Made in Heaven, and I wanted to enter the contest because I love baking cookies. But there was more to it than that." I met Dad's gaze. "I wanted to win because of the shopping spree." Dad raised a questioning eyebrow, so I explained about the grand-prize shopping spree to the Baking and Culinary Arts Depot. "We could get a head start on supplies for our restaurant. You've both been so busy. I knew you wouldn't have as much time to shop for supplies, so I'd take care of it for you. I figured as soon as you talked to Mrs. Yang, you'd be putting an offer on the space, and I wanted to help—"

"Oh, beti," Dad whispered, his eyes widening. "This was about our restaurant?" He glanced at Mom, who'd covered her mouth with her hand.

I nodded. "It means so much to you. You've been talking about it for as long as I can remember."

Dad's eyes misted over, and he pulled me into another hug. It took him a few moments of gruff throat clearing before he could finally speak. "I'm so proud of you, Mina. And we love you so much." Mom nodded and smiled at me. "But even with a shopping spree, we wouldn't be opening our restaurant anytime soon."

"But—but I thought—"

Dad held up a hand. "We could open, yes. Anytime we choose." He gave me an apologetic smile. "We could've opened months ago if we'd wanted. But I haven't called Mrs. Yang about buying her space."

"But why *not*?" I asked.

"Now isn't the right time."

I stared at him in confusion. "I don't understand, Dad. It's your dream."

"*Our* dream," Mom said. "I know you think I'm not happy about a restaurant. But that's not true. I want it, too. Someday."

Dad nodded, squeezing Mom's hand. "The restaurant is just one dream out of many. You are also one of our dreams. So are your sister and brother. There will come a time for the restaurant, but our schedules are too overwhelming. The babies still need so much of our attention and care. And that's okay." He smiled. "Our restaurant *will* happen. When it's right for all of us. Together."

"Oh." Understanding washed over me. No wonder Dad had held off on calling Mrs. Yang. I sighed. "I thought if I could just do this *one* thing, it could fix everything."

Dad chuckled. "You and your fixing. Life isn't something to be fixed. It's something to be *lived*. And enjoyed . . . just as it is."

"And right now," Mom chimed in, "we only have time for one more life-changing event."

I gasped, my heart lurching. "Are you having another baby?" I squeaked.

Dad's laugh boomed through the kitchen. "No!" He raised his eyes to the ceiling. "Two is more than enough!"

"I meant the Cookie Crumbles contest," Mom wheezed through her own laughter. "We've decided that you can go."

My heart galloped in my chest as I stared at them. "What?"

Dad nodded. "We'll bring the twins with us to Seattle. Your mom and I will take turns watching them while you do the bake-off." His eyes sparkled. "It'll be an adventure. We'll figure it out."

"Oh." A thousand thoughts tumbled through my brain, and guilt stung my chest. "Oh," I said again, at a total loss. *Now* what? My parents were doing exactly what I'd hoped they'd do days ago. They were giving me permission to take part in the Cookie Crumbles contest. Except that—*argh*—it was too late. I'd already lied to them about the whole thing.

Mom frowned as she took in the dismay on my face. "What is it, Mina?" she asked worriedly. "We thought you'd be so happy."

"I am!" I said. "I mean, I—" I dropped my head, covering my face with my hands. I had to tell them the entire truth, but once I did, they'd forbid me from going to the contest for real. My stomach soured, and my palms grew slick with cold sweat. "The thing is . . . I have to tell you something." I swallowed, dreading what was coming next. "You're not going to like it."

Mom and Dad exchanged concerned glances.

"Go on." Dad's voice was low and somber.

Every sound in the room was drowned out by the pounding of my heart. I clasped my hands together under the table to keep them from visibly shaking. "I'm so, so sorry," I began in a tremulous voice. "But I—I lied to you. When you told me that I wasn't allowed to go to Seattle for the contest, I . . ." I sucked in a bolstering breath, then let my next words pour out in a flood. "I signed Mom's name on the online contest forms so that I could still go!"

For an excruciating moment, neither of my parents moved. Time seemed frozen. Then Dad closed his eyes. When he opened his eyes again, they were full of shock and dismay.

"You . . . you forged your mother's name?" He shook his head, frowning at me. "And you were going to . . . what? Run away to Seattle without telling us? Disappear?"

I shrugged as my body sagged inward. Dad's disappointment

was a needle piercing my chest. "I hadn't worked out all the plans yet," I whispered. "I was going to take a bus to Seattle, and then figure it out from there."

"How could you even *think* such a thing?" Mom cried. "To disappear without a word to us! You could have been kidnapped in Seattle, or lost goodness-knows-where. We would've been out of our minds worrying!"

"But I didn't do it!" I said. "I *didn't* run away. And . . . I probably wouldn't have even gone through with it."

Dad glowered at me. "Probably?" he repeated. "You deliberately disobeyed us. And you lied."

"I'm so, *so* sorry! Please try to understand," I pleaded. "I was mad at you. Maybe I was even mad at Amul and Banita, too, which I know doesn't make sense. Because, I mean, they don't even have teeth yet! Or much hair, either! And . . . who gets mad at babies anyway?"

The corner of Mom's mouth twitched, and I wondered if she might be trying to stifle a smile. A second later, though, her expression had resumed its sternness.

"I love Amul and Banita," I went on, "but everything has been harder since they were born. You wouldn't even listen when I tried to tell you about the contest." I stared at the dining room table. "What I did was totally wrong. And I don't think I deserve to participate in the contest anymore. I'll email Cookie Crumbles to tell them I can't go. Right now. If you want me to."

With those last words, I deflated. There was nothing else I could say. I'd been honest, and now I'd have to accept the consequences. I sat motionless, struggling to accept my inevitable fate.

After a few excruciating seconds of silence, the baby monitor crackled to life with the sound of crying.

"I'll go!" I jumped up from the table before either of my parents could utter a sound. Relieved to escape the tension, I took the stairs two at a time to the nursery. Banita was fussing while Amul lay sleeping soundly beside her. I scooped up my sister, and she instantly quieted as I bounced her gently in my arms.

"Your big sister is in big, *big* trouble," I whispered to her in the darkness. "They'll probably go easier on you, because you're the youngest. But don't worry." I stroked the soft black curls crowning her forehead. "I promise not to hold it against you."

I sat down in the nearby rocker, and we swayed together, her tiny body pressed warmly against my own. I closed my eyes, trying not to think about the many punishments my parents might be devising for me downstairs at that very moment. Instead, I hummed one of my favorite Hindi lullabies Mom had sung to me when I was little. I might have even dozed off for a few minutes, soothed by Banita's butterfly-soft, rhythmic breathing.

When I opened my eyes again, Mom was standing in the nursery doorway. A shaft of light falling from the hallway illuminated the gentle smile on her face.

"Thank you," she whispered, taking Banita from my arms to lay her back down in the crib. Stirring just long enough to find Amul's hand with her own, Banita drifted off to sleep, her forehead inches from our brother's.

Mom and I tiptoed from the room and made our way downstairs, where Dad was waiting. "Your mother and I have talked it over," he said solemnly, "and we've made a decision."

I nodded, waiting for my nervousness to spike. It didn't, though, and I realized that, no matter what my parents decided my punishment should be, I'd be okay. *We'd* be okay. Now that they'd listened to me, at last, and seemed to understand what they hadn't been able to before, the contest didn't seem as important anymore.

"What you did was wrong," Dad went on, "and you'll be grounded for the next week, which means no cell phone or screen time . . ." He held out his hand, and I pulled my phone from my back pocket and placed it in his open palm. "No after-school activities except your job at the cookie shop. Straight home after that." He looked at me sternly from under furrowed brows. "Understood?"

"Yes." I clasped and unclasped my hands, anxious to have the rest of it over and done with. But to my surprise, Dad gave a single nod, as if the discussion was finished. He turned away, opening the freezer and rummaging through, no doubt in search of his favorite mango kulfi for dessert.

"Um . . ." My pulse quickened. I couldn't believe I was actually going to bring this up, but I had to. "What about the Cookie Crumbles contest? Should I send an email now?"

Dad found the kulfi, popped its lid, and began eating it straight from the container with his spoon.

"Ah, the contest. Yes." He lifted his spoon in the air, and I held my breath. "Tomorrow, you—"

"Tell them I can't participate," I finished for him. I tried to keep a steady, brave face, but a small quaver in my voice betrayed my sadness. "Yes."

I turned away, but Dad called my name to stop me. "I was going to say . . ." He swallowed another spoonful of kulfi. "Tomorrow you and I will go over the travel details and make sure our hotel room is confirmed." A smile crossed his face. "That is, if you still want to go—"

"I want to go!" I shrieked, and threw myself into his arms, nearly knocking him backward with the force of my hug.

He chuckled as Mom joined in the hug, our arms wrapped snugly around one another.

"Thank you!" I said to both of them. "Thank you so much."

Dad drew me away from his chest, wagging a finger. "One thing, beti. *If* you win, you understand that our restaurant will still have to wait. It has to be the right time for all of us as a family. Someday, Mina, but not just yet."

I nodded. "I understand." I grinned, my mind unspooling a happy thread of ideas. "I can think of a million things to buy on the shopping spree for us to use at home instead! A tandoor, a new mixer . . ."

His and Mom's laughter brightened the entire kitchen. Then Mom made a grab for Dad's spoon. "Are you going to share with the rest of us or not?" she teased.

"I'm on it, Mom," I said, trying to snatch the spoon as Dad hid it behind his back.

Then all three of us were laughing. My fight with Flynn was still a splinter in my heart. But I vowed not to think about that tonight. Tonight, I'd relish the refreshing, tangy taste of mango kulfi, and the love of my parents. Tonight, that would be more than enough.

Chapter Thirteen

The next morning when I woke up, rain was hammering the window and the sky was a bleak, heavy gray. Still, the world seemed a brighter, more beautiful place. Even after I came downstairs to find Mom frantically hurrying to leave for work, and Dad staring forlornly into a burnt pot of Cream of Wheat as Amul and Banita fussed for their bottles, I didn't let the chaos frustrate me. Instead, I scrubbed the lumpy goop out of the pot, warmed bottles for the babies, and poured Dad a fresh cup of coffee while he changed his spit-up-soiled shirt.

"Remember. It won't always be this hard," I said to him when he reappeared in the kitchen, echoing his words from the night before.

He laughed. "I may have spoken too soon." When I grabbed my schoolbag, he stopped me. "Don't forget. Home straight after—"

"After school," I interjected. "I know." Then some of my cheeriness faltered. *Flynn*, I thought. *I'm going to have to see Flynn.* The mere thought of running into him at school, let alone working with him at the shop, brought my anger and hurt to the surface all over again. How could I possibly keep working with him? Helping Mr. Winston out yesterday had only been possible for me because Flynn hadn't been there.

"Everything okay?" Dad peered at my face in concern.

I shook my thoughts away. "Fine. I'm just . . . not sure how much longer I want to work at A Batch Made in Heaven. That's all."

"And why is that?" Dad's eyebrows skyrocketed. "You've loved working there. And doesn't the mentorship program last through the end of October?"

"I did love working there, but I don't want to work with

anyone who—" I stopped myself, then shrugged, trying to seem casual. "There's only a week left in the program. I'm sure Mr. Imari would understand if you and I talked to him about skipping my last Monday there." I grabbed a banana from the fruit basket on the counter. "We could just say that you need my help with the twins."

Dad contemplated this, frowning. "That may well be true, but I won't have you using that as an excuse to avoid something"—he gave me a pointed look—"or *someone*, simply because you've had a conflict."

My brow crinkled. "It's not like that." But I couldn't explain. It made me too upset. "I've got to go," I said.

I tried to walk past my dad, but he motioned for me to wait. His eyes silently dissected my facade of nonchalance. "Does this have anything to do with Mr. Winston's son? Flynn? Isn't that his name?"

"Wha— No! Why?" I dropped my eyes as my cheeks burned.

Dad put his hands on his hips. "Because I believe he's been pacing the sidewalk in front of our house for the last hour."

"He—he has?" I stammered. My eyes flew to the kitchen's bay window, but there was no sign of Flynn outside. I stiffened. "Well, it doesn't matter if he *was* here. He's not now. And I don't care, anyway."

"I'm not sure what's going on," Dad said, "but whatever it is, hiding from it won't do any good." He kissed the top of my head, then urged me toward the door, a smile playing around the corners of his mouth. "Have a good day at school. And know that I will not be looking out the kitchen window for at least . . ." He checked his watch. "Ten minutes." His eyes glinted.

"Dad." I rolled my eyes, exasperated now. "You're not making any sense."

He chuckled, then held up both hands, fingers splayed out. "Ten minutes."

I shook my head in confusion but waved goodbye and, after putting on my raincoat and grabbing my umbrella, opened the front door. I lifted my foot to step onto the porch, but then stumbled as I narrowly avoided a square, flat box on the doorstep.

For Mina was scrawled in smeared, rain-dampened marker across the lid. I recognized Flynn's messy handwriting instantly.

I bent down and lifted the lid of the box, my heart somersaulting. Inside the box was a cookie the size of an extra-large pizza with words written across it in chocolate icing:

Without you, I would crumble.

I laughed in spite of myself.

"Is it safe for me to show my face?" came Flynn's voice from behind me. I turned to find him standing on our lawn in the pouring rain, drenched from head to toe.

For a second, I was at a complete loss for words. Finally, I motioned to the cookie and mumbled, "How'd you know I wouldn't stomp it into a million pieces?"

"I didn't." He gave a short laugh. "But I was feeling optimistic."

I stared at him, anger and longing playing tug-of-war with my heart. "You're completely drenched," I managed awkwardly.

"It doesn't matter," he said. "I was going to leave, but . . . I couldn't." His freckled cheeks were a brighter red than I'd ever seen them, whether from the chilly air or embarrassment I didn't know. I couldn't help noticing how vulnerable (and cute) he looked at this moment. Rain dripped from his curls, and he was twisting the bottom of his soaking hoodie nervously in his hands.

But I would not be confused by his cuteness right now, I told myself. Or by the undeniably sweet gesture of the cookie. I was still mad at him. I stiffened with resolve, folding my arms across my chest. "What are you doing here?" I asked.

A small, sad smile flickered across his face. "Okay . . ." He sighed out a long breath. "You're not going to make this easy for me." His indigo eyes settled on mine. "I'm sorry. For everything I said. I was completely out of line."

"Yes." I nodded.

"I should never have jumped to conclusions, especially because they went against everything I knew about you."

I nodded again. "True."

"Kalli showed up at my house last night," he went on. "She told me about the reporter coming to the shop that night you and I were baking. She explained what happened with my recipe book. And I know you helped my dad at the shop yesterday, too . . ."

"So that's why you're here?" I frowned. "Because Kalli and your dad told you that I was innocent?"

"No!" He shook his head. "Even before I knew all of that, I tried calling you to apologize. And I sent you a bunch of text messages last night, but you didn't return any of them."

"Oh." Some of my anger eased. "My parents took my phone away. But . . . you didn't come to the store after school. You disappeared! And your dad—"

"I know. I went to the archery range to blow off some steam with Trent and Will. I couldn't deal with the shop yesterday. Just once, I wanted Dad to sweat a little over the recipes. I'd been so frustrated for so long and . . ." He pushed a hand through his wet hair. "Everything just came to a head. When I finally got home last night, my dad and I talked over everything. I told him I want to spend less time at the shop. And that I want to join the archery team."

"Wow," I said. "Sounds like a big night."

"It was. But Dad surprised me. He took what I said in stride, and told me that he agreed. That it was time for him to either step up with inventing recipes of his own, or give some serious thought to the future of the shop." He shrugged. "I don't know what will happen, but I feel . . . relieved. It's not all on me anymore, you know?"

I nodded.

"But . . ." He hesitated. "I know I behaved like a total jerk, and I wouldn't blame you if you hated me and never wanted to see me again."

He turned to head down the sidewalk, and the splinter in my heart broke free.

"Flynn, wait!" I jogged across the lawn after him. The rain was cold and stinging, but I barely noticed. "I don't. Hate you."

"Y-you don't?" he whispered, his eyes hopeful. I shook my head. "I've spent such a long time on the defensive. I forgot, for a second, what an amazing person you are, and how you could never, ever do what I accused you of."

"Right on all counts." I smiled. "I *am* pretty amazing. And don't you ever forget it again."

He laughed in relief. "I never will."

I felt at my core that he'd made me a promise he'd never break.

"I'm so glad we've made u—" I caught myself before I finished the words "made up," heat flashing over my face. "I mean, that we're friends again," I backtracked. "Because now I can ask you to come along to the Cookie Crumbles bake-off with me. My parents said I could bring a couple of friends along. If . . ." My pulse accelerated. "If you want to come with me, that is."

He didn't miss a beat. "Of course I want to come!" he exclaimed, his eyes bright. "I'll be the one cheering the loudest when you win."

I laughed. "Winning is a long shot, but I'll gladly take a cheering section."

"Not a long shot." Flynn held my gaze. "Not for you." He stepped closer, looking suddenly serious. "But, Mina, there's still a problem. I'm not sure how we can stay friends."

"Wh-why not?" I asked, shock and confusion gutting me. I dropped my eyes as every bitter emotion threatened to consume me all over again. Then I gasped as he touched his finger to my chin, lifting my face up.

"Because," he whispered, "I'm hoping we can be more than friends."

Realization swept over me. My heart was pounding a happy tune that drowned out the hammering of the rain as I smiled up at him. "Well, there's only one way to fix this."

His eyes widened in a question, and I answered them by bringing my lips to his in a soft, rain-sweetened kiss. My arms encircled his neck, and he held my waist. For one breathless moment, we were floating. When I finally, slowly opened my eyes, Flynn was grinning at me.

"That is one great solution," he whispered.

"I agree," I whispered. I glanced back toward the front porch, where the cookie box sat waiting. "You know, I didn't eat breakfast yet. And I'm suddenly craving cookies."

His eyes followed mine. "There's nothing like dessert for breakfast."

"Breakfast for two, then?" I asked, and he nodded. I slid my hand into his, and together, smiling, we walked through the rain.

Chapter Fourteen

"Time's almost up, bakers!" Ms. Sheldon announced.

Oh no, I thought, checking the oven as my heart raced. This was it.

When we'd begun livestreaming the Cookie Crumbles bake-off a little over an hour ago, I'd been acutely aware of the cameras. The enormous kitchen was outfitted with five baking stations that had everything each of us contestants needed to bake our cookies, including individual ovens, refrigerators, and mixers, and dozens of ingredients. The lights positioned over each baking station were blindingly bright and hot, and the chef's coat I had to wear only made me hotter.

Once the countdown had begun, though, I'd forgotten all about the lights and cameras. Instead, I thought of Flynn, Kalli, my parents, and the twins—all watching from the green room off camera. I sensed them cheering me on. Back home in Oyster Cove, Jane and Fabs were watching the livestream on YouTube, too. So many people I cared about were with me in spirit.

This is my moment, I'd decided then. *My moment to do what I love best—bake.* So that's what I'd done. And in just a minute, my latest cookie invention was about to come out of the oven and be presented to the world.

Now Ms. Sheldon offered me an encouraging smile, as if she sensed my nervousness. Not only was she the emcee for today's bake-off, she was also one of the official Cookie Crumbles recipe inventors. The other four contestants and I had spent yesterday taking a fun sightseeing walk around downtown Seattle with her. We'd gotten our photos taken at the Space Needle and in

Chihuly Garden, and then, afterward, we'd toured the Cookie Crumbles factory. The factory was enormous, and even though it was exciting seeing the gigantic mixers and huge vats of creaming eggs and sugar, it all felt a little impersonal. But then we'd gotten a firsthand look at the Invention Kitchen, where Ms. Sheldon and a couple of other bakers experimented with recipes to find the perfect ones. The Invention Kitchen was where Ms. Sheldon said the real magic happened—where bakers like her could unleash the full power of their creativity. Finally, we were taken to the "Tasting Room," where we'd been able to taste-test three brand-new cookie prototypes that were being considered for distribution to grocery stores nationwide.

Ms. Sheldon had an impressive talent for being able to identify ingredients in a cookie solely by smell. She'd actually demonstrated this in the Invention Kitchen, naming every single ingredient for a batch of cookies that was baking in the oven. Later, I was even brave enough to show her that I could do the same thing when I tasted a cookie.

"Incredible," she'd said admiringly when I'd guessed every

ingredient correctly. "Not many people would've been able to pick up on the subtle hint of sage in that shortbread cookie. What a wonderful gift."

I'd glowed at her comment. But now, after spending the last hour creating my own cookie recipe under her watchful eye, I wanted more than anything to prove to her that I could bake even better than I could taste-test.

I grabbed the oven mitts from the counter and turned to my oven, where, through the glass door, I could see my cookies were chocolate brown and baked to perfection. I slid them from the oven and set them on the counter to cool for a minute before carefully placing them on a platter to present to the judges. I glanced at the other four contestants as they took their cookies from the ovens, too. They were all kids my age. Yesterday, we'd gotten to know one another a little during the factory tour, and they all seemed nice, and talented, too. Right now, though, they looked just as nervous as I felt.

We all started when the final buzzer sounded loudly through the kitchen.

"Okay, bakers." Ms. Sheldon walked past our stations to review our finished cookies. "Let's see what spectacular cookie creations you've made today."

Two other judges, including the CEO of Cookie Crumbles Inc., joined Ms. Sheldon, stopping in front of Rosa Flores's station first. Rosa explained that her cookie was a unique spin on Mexican wedding cookies, made with orange zest and saffron in addition to the traditional almonds and vanilla extract. All three of the judges praised her use of the orange zest and agreed that the cookies were tangy and fun, even though they'd come out a little dry.

I held my breath as Nigel, Saadia, and Kate all presented their cookies for taste testing. Then, before I knew it, Ms. Sheldon was standing before me with the other judges.

"Mina." Ms. Sheldon smiled. "Tell us about your cookie."

My heart was pounding so hard I feared it might stop completely, but somehow, I managed a smile. "My cookie is a fusion of flavors. I used Nutella, chopped hazelnuts and dates, and smoked sweet paprika in the batter, and then stuffed each cookie with a Lindt hazelnut truffle."

"What an unusual list of ingredients," remarked Mrs. Dietrich, the CEO. "My mouth is watering already." She picked up one of the cookies, then hesitated. "Does your cookie have a name?"

I nodded. "I Chews You." I smiled. "It's named for someone special I know who started out a little raw but, in the end, turned out perfectly sweet."

Ms. Sheldon nodded knowingly. "In my experience, the very best recipes are the ones that come from the heart." Then she took a big bite of one of the cookies as Mrs. Dietrich and the other judge did the same.

I watched in suspense as they chewed methodically, and then felt a wave of relief as slow smiles spread over their faces.

"Unexpected and delicious," Ms. Sheldon said.

"Delightfully surprising," Mrs. Dietrich pronounced, "and so rich and satisfying."

"Baked to perfection," Mr. Walsh, the third judge, added.

Joy raced through me. I clasped my hands together and grinned. "Thank you," I managed to say. I bounced on my toes in elation when what I really wanted to do was jump up and down whooping wildly.

Ms. Sheldon stepped back to take all the contestants into her gaze. "The other judges and I will cast our final votes while you wait in the green room with your families. We'll call you back in a few minutes to announce the Cookie Crumbles champion."

We nodded, and then, tripping over ourselves with relief and excitement and congratulating each other on jobs well done, we made our way out of the kitchen and into the adjoining green room.

I'd barely crossed the threshold before Kalli and Flynn threw their arms around me in a double hug.

"You were amazing!" Kalli shrieked. "So professional the whole time."

"Phenomenal," Flynn added with a smile, and then my parents were moving in for hugs. Amul and Banita got in on the action, too, strapped as they were into baby carriers against my parents' chests.

"We're so proud of you, beti," Dad whispered, his eyes misting over. "This is a wonderful accomplishment."

"Thanks, Dad." I snuggled into my parents' embrace. "I'm so glad we could all be here together."

"We are, too." Mom kissed my forehead, and then Amul began fussing. "Bottle time," she said, and Dad nodded, both of them retreating to the couch where the diaper bag, with bottles galore, was waiting.

"You're totally going to win," Kalli whispered to me. She squeezed my hand before rejoining my parents.

I glanced up at Flynn, who was gazing down at me, looking cuter than ever.

"The new cookie recipe looks fantastic," he said. "And I especially like the name."

I smiled back at him. "I named it for you."

"Thank you." He slid his arms around my waist, whispering in my ear, "I choose you, too." He pressed his cheek to mine, and then our lips found each other in a sweet, soft kiss.

The world around us faded into blissful oblivion, and Flynn and I might've stayed in our own magical universe if not for Kalli urgently tugging my elbow.

"Mina, it's time!" She motioned to the other contestants exiting the room. "You have to get back to the kitchen. They're going to announce the winner."

"Omigosh!" I breathed, straightening. "Okay. I'm ready."

With my family waving me out the door and Flynn blowing me a kiss, I hurried after the other contestants and back into the bright lights of the Cookie Crumbles kitchen. As the contestants and I stood together, hand in hand, waiting for the news, I smiled into the cameras and an unexpected calm swept over me. I knew beyond any doubt that I'd done the best I could. My family, best friend, and boyfriend (!) were backstage waiting for me, and they were here for me and would always be here for me, whether I won this contest or not. Regardless of what happened, my life was sweeter than any cookie I could ever bake, and that was all that mattered.

A Batch Made in Heaven
Cookie Recipes

There is nothing quite as comforting (or delicious)
as warm, melt-in-your-mouth cookies straight out
of the oven. Just the scent of fresh-baked cookies can bring
a smile to someone's face. Give Flynn's and Mina's recipes a
try, and you'll be snuggled under a blanket with a cup
of warm cocoa and a plate of ooey-gooey cookie goodness
in no time. Remember to always have adult supervision
when using an electric mixer, stovetop, or oven.
Melted butter can be very hot—be sure to have an adult help
remove it from the microwave. Before starting any baking,
remember to check the recipes for allergen concerns and
make the appropriate substitutions.

To make any or all of these cookies, you'll need a
microwave, two to three medium or large mixing bowls, a
handheld or stand mixer, one or two nonstick baking sheets,
parchment paper, oven mitts, measuring cups
and spoons, and a spatula.

I Like You Choco-lot
Garam Masala Cookies

For this recipe, instead of baking sheets, you will
use a cupcake baking tin and cupcake liners.

INGREDIENTS:
- 1 stick unsalted butter, melted
- 1 egg at room temperature
- 1 tsp vanilla extract
- 1 shot espresso or pinch of espresso powder (optional)
- ½ cup packed dark brown sugar
- ⅓ cup white granulated sugar
- 1 cup flour
- ½ tsp baking soda
- ½ tsp salt
- ½ cup dark, unsweetened baking cocoa
  (like Hershey's Special Dark Cocoa)
- 1 tsp garam masala spice blend (or to taste)
- ¾ cup semisweet chocolate morsels (like Nestle's Toll House)
- 12 Amul Chocominis truffles (can be found
  online or at specialty grocery stores)
  (or, if you can't find Amul chocolates, you can use Lindt
  chocolate truffles instead)

DIRECTIONS:
Preheat your oven to 350° Fahrenheit. Line a cupcake
baking tin with cupcake liners. Using a microwave and
microwaveable bowl, carefully melt the butter and set aside.
Or leave the butter out at room temperature for a few hours
to soften naturally.

In a medium mixing bowl, combine egg, vanilla, espresso, brown sugar, and granulated sugar. Using a handheld or electric stand mixer, beat the egg mixture for approximately 1 minute. Then mix in melted butter.

In a separate bowl, combine flour, baking soda, salt, baking cocoa, and garam masala spices. Slowly add the dry ingredients to the wet ingredients, mixing as you go. Once your dough is well-blended, stir in the chocolate morsels.

Fill each cupcake liner three-quarters full of dough, and then press an unwrapped truffle into the center of each ball of dough.

Bake the cookies for 15 to 20 minutes. The truffle in the center will melt, and when the cookies are finished baking, they'll resemble mini chocolate lava cakes. Be sure to ask your adult assistant for help removing the cookies from the oven. Allow the cookies to cool for 10 to 15 minutes before serving. This recipe makes about 12 cookies.

Candy Bar Crush Cookies

INGREDIENTS:

- 2 sticks unsalted butter, softened
- 2 eggs at room temperature
- ½ tsp vanilla extract
- ¾ cup light brown sugar
- ¼ cup white granulated sugar
- 2½ cups flour
- 1 tsp baking soda
- 1 tsp baking powder
- 2 cups chopped candy bars of your choice (for my version of these cookies, I use 4 Kit Kats, 2 Snickers, 2 Heath, 3 Twix, and 2 Butterfingers)
- 12 to 16 unwrapped Rolo candies (for the center filling of your cookies)

DIRECTIONS:

Preheat your oven to 375° Fahrenheit. Line a nonstick baking sheet with parchment paper. (Note: These cookies have a very sticky, gooey center, so parchment paper is a MUST if you don't want your cookies sticking to your baking sheet.)

Using a microwave and microwaveable bowl, carefully soften the butter and set aside. Or leave the butter out at room temperature for a few hours to soften naturally.

In a medium mixing bowl, combine eggs, vanilla, brown sugar, and granulated sugar.

Using a handheld or electric stand mixer, beat the egg mixture for approximately 1 minute. Then mix in softened butter, beating until creamy. In a separate bowl, combine flour, baking soda, and baking powder. Slowly add the dry ingredients to the wet ingredients, mixing as you go.

Once your dough is well-blended, stir in your chopped candy bar pieces. To make extra-large, gooey-chewy cookies, place large, heaping spoonfuls of dough on your baking sheet.

You may only be able to fit 6 to 8 cookie dough balls on a baking sheet at a time. Using a butter-coated teaspoon, create a crater in the dough at the center of each cookie. Gently press a Rolo into the top of each cookie.

Using your fingers, pinch the sides of the cookie dough ball to cover up the Rolo with dough. Bake the cookies for 12 to 15 minutes, until golden brown around the edges.

Allow the cookies to cool for 10 to 15 minutes before serving. This recipe makes 10 to 12 cookies, depending on how large you make them.

Cheesecake and Chill Cookies

INGREDIENTS:

- 2 sticks unsalted butter, softened
- 2 eggs at room temperature
- 2 tbsp vanilla extract
- 1 cup light brown sugar
- ⅓ cup white granulated sugar
- 2½ cups flour
- 1 tsp baking soda
- ½ tsp baking powder
- 1 tsp salt
- 1 cup white chocolate chip morsels (like Ghirardelli)
- 1 cup chopped iced animal cookies (like Mother's or Stauffer's cookies)
- 1 large slice of store-bought or homemade cheesecake (Junior's Cheesecake can be found in many grocery stores premade)

DIRECTIONS:

Preheat your oven to 350° Fahrenheit. Line a nonstick baking sheet with parchment paper. (Note: These cookies have a cheesecake-stuffed center, so parchment paper is a MUST if you don't want your cookies sticking to your baking sheet.)

Using a microwave and microwaveable bowl, carefully soften the butter and set aside. Or leave the butter out at room temperature for a few hours to soften naturally.

In a medium mixing bowl, combine eggs, vanilla, brown sugar, and granulated sugar.

Using a handheld or electric stand mixer, beat the egg mixture for approximately 1 minute. Then mix in softened butter, beating until creamy. In a separate bowl, combine flour, baking soda, baking powder, and salt. Slowly, add the dry ingredients to the wet ingredients, mixing as you go.

Once your dough is well-blended, stir in your chopped animal cookies and white chocolate chips. To make extra-large, gooey-chewy cookies, place large, heaping spoonfuls of dough on the baking sheet.

You may only be able to fit 6 to 8 cookie dough balls on a baking sheet at a time. Using a butter-coated teaspoon, create a crater in the dough at the center of each cookie. Gently press a chunk of cheesecake into the crater.

Using your fingers, pinch the sides of the cookie dough ball to cover up the cheesecake with dough. Bake the cookies for 12 to 15 minutes, until golden brown around the edges.

Allow the cookies to cool for 10 to 15 minutes before serving. This recipe makes 10 to 12 cookies, depending on how large you make them.

Cookie Monster Cookies

INGREDIENTS:

- 2 sticks unsalted butter, softened
- 2 eggs at room temperature
- 1 tsp vanilla extract
- ¾ cup light brown sugar
- ½ cup white granulated sugar
- 2½ cups flour
- 1 tsp baking soda
- 1 tsp baking powder
- ½ tsp salt
- ⅓ cup chopped cornflakes
- ⅓ cup crushed potato chips
- ⅓ cup chopped small pretzel sticks
- ⅓ cup white chocolate morsels (like Ghirardelli)
- ⅓ cup semisweet chocolate morsels (like Nestle Toll House)
- ⅓ cup toffee bits (like Heath baking toffee bits)

DIRECTIONS:

Preheat your oven to 375° Fahrenheit. Line a nonstick baking sheet with parchment paper.

Using a microwave and microwaveable bowl, carefully soften the butter and set aside. Or leave the butter out at room temperature for a few hours to soften naturally.

In a medium mixing bowl, combine eggs, vanilla, brown sugar, and granulated sugar.

Using a handheld or electric stand mixer, beat the egg mixture for approximately 1 minute. Then mix in softened butter, beating until creamy. In a separate bowl, combine flour, baking soda, baking powder, and salt. Slowly add the dry ingredients to the wet ingredients, mixing as you go.

Once your dough is well-blended, stir in your cornflakes, potato chips, pretzels, white and dark chocolate morsels, and toffee bits. To make extra-large cookies like the kind baked at A Batch Made in Heaven, place large, heaping spoonfuls of dough on your baking sheet.

You may only be able to fit 6 to 8 cookie dough balls on a baking sheet at a time. Bake the cookies for 12 to 15 minutes, until golden brown around the edges.

Allow the cookies to cool for 5 to 10 minutes before serving. This recipe makes 10 to 12 cookies, depending on how large you make them.

Have you read them all? Don't miss a single scrumptious book from Suzanne Nelson!

Alicia Ramirez loves baking cake pops at her dad's bakery, Say It With Flour. But when a sleek coffee shop moves in across the street, can she win a baking contest against the owner's son?

Tessa Kostas loves working in her aunt's trendy food truck . . . until arrogant (and cute) Asher starts helping with the BLTs. Can Tessa and Asher set aside their differences and work together to help save the truck? Now a Hallmark Channel Original Movie!

Emery Mason isn't a fan of the holidays; her parents are making her work as an elf in their photo booth at the mall this year. Can Alex Perez, who works at the hot cocoa stand nearby, help Em embrace the magic of the season?

When Lise Santos stumbles into a bakery's midnight taste test, she meets a cute boy but doesn't learn his name. With the help of some friends and delicious macarons, can she find him again?

When tween heartthrob Cabe Sadler begins filming his next movie in an NYC doughnut shop, he literally runs into Sheyda Nazari and casts her as his co-star. But Sheyda isn't used to the spotlight. Can she overcome her stage fright and get to know the real Cabe?

Malie Analu helps out at her mom's ice cream shop, but her true love is ballet. Then Alonzo, a new boy from Italy, promises Malie a trade: if he can help out with the ice cream, Malie can take lessons from his mom, a famed ballerina. But is their deal doomed to spin out of control?

Dacey Culpepper Biel comes from a long line of pie bakers . . . but she does not have the baking gift. Can a long-lost family recipe, a social media influencer, and an old rival save her family's legacy?

Bria Muller is stuck on her aunt and uncle's dairy farm for the summer, and she is not happy about it. The one thing she's good at is mixing up over-the-top milk shakes in the creamery. Will Bria ever fit into country life?

Nadine and Daniel have been best friends pretty much since birth, and always make time for their after-school lattes. But what will happen when Daniel falls head over heels in like with the new girl?

Have you read all the wish books?

- [ ] *Clementine for Christmas* by Daphne Benedis-Grab
- [ ] *Carols and Crushes* by Natalie Blitt
- [ ] *Snow One Like You* by Natalie Blitt
- [ ] *Allie, First at Last* by Angela Cervantes
- [ ] *Gaby, Lost and Found* by Angela Cervantes
- [ ] *Lety Out Loud* by Angela Cervantes
- [ ] *Keep It Together, Keiko Carter* by Debbi Michiko Florence
- [ ] *Alpaca My Bags* by Jenny Goebel
- [ ] *Pigture Perfect* by Jenny Goebel
- [ ] *Sit, Stay, Love* by J. J. Howard
- [ ] *Pugs and Kisses* by J. J. Howard
- [ ] *Pugs in a Blanket* by J. J. Howard
- [ ] *The Love Pug* by J. J. Howard
- [ ] *Girls Just Wanna Have Pugs* by J. J. Howard
- [ ] *The Boy Project* by Kami Kinard
- [ ] *Best Friend Next Door* by Carolyn Mackler
- [ ] *11 Birthdays* by Wendy Mass
- [ ] *Finally* by Wendy Mass
- [ ] *13 Gifts* by Wendy Mass
- [ ] *The Last Present* by Wendy Mass
- [ ] *Graceful* by Wendy Mass
- [ ] *Twice Upon a Time: Beauty and the Beast, the Only One Who Didn't Run Away* by Wendy Mass
- [ ] *Twice Upon a Time: Rapunzel, the One with All the Hair* by Wendy Mass

- ☐ *Twice Upon a Time: Robin Hood, the One Who Looked Good in Green* by Wendy Mass

- ☐ *Twice Upon a Time: Sleeping Beauty, the One Who Took the Really Long Nap* by Wendy Mass

- ☐ *Blizzard Besties* by Yamile Saied Méndez

- ☐ *Random Acts of Kittens* by Yamile Saied Méndez

- ☐ *Wish Upon a Stray* by Yamile Saied Méndez

- ☐ *Playing Cupid* by Jenny Meyerhoff

- ☐ *Cake Pop Crush* by Suzanne Nelson

- ☐ *Macarons at Midnight* by Suzanne Nelson

- ☐ *Hot Cocoa Hearts* by Suzanne Nelson

- ☐ *You're Bacon Me Crazy* by Suzanne Nelson

- ☐ *Donut Go Breaking My Heart* by Suzanne Nelson

- ☐ *Sundae My Prince Will Come* by Suzanne Nelson

- ☐ *I Only Have Pies for You* by Suzanne Nelson

- ☐ *Shake It Off* by Suzanne Nelson

- ☐ *Pumpkin Spice Up Your Life* by Suzanne Nelson

- ☐ *A Batch Made in Heaven* by Suzanne Nelson

- ☐ *Confectionately Yours: Save the Cupcake!* by Lisa Papademetriou

- ☐ *My Secret Guide to Paris* by Lisa Schroeder

- ☐ *Sealed with a Secret* by Lisa Schroeder

- ☐ *Switched at Birthday* by Natalie Standiford

- ☐ *The Only Girl in School* by Natalie Standiford

- ☐ *Clique Here* by Anna Staniszewski

- ☐ *Double Clique* by Anna Staniszewski

- ☐ *Once Upon a Cruise* by Anna Staniszewski

- ☐ *Deep Down Popular* by Phoebe Stone

- ☐ *Meow or Never* by Jazz Taylor

- ☐ *Revenge of the Flower Girls* by Jennifer Ziegler

- ☐ *Revenge of the Angels* by Jennifer Ziegler

Read the latest books!

pumpkin spice up your life

a batch made in heaven

TWICE UPON A TIME
Robin Hood
WANTED
The One Who Looked Good in Green
WENDY MASS

angela cervantes
LETY OUT LOUD

girls just wanna have pugs
j.j. howard

alpaca my bags
Jenny Goebel

pigture perfect
Jenny Goebel

Wish UPON A Stray
YAMILE SAIED MÉNDEZ

meow or never

Anna Staniszewski
CLIQUE HERE

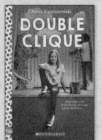

Anna Staniszewski
DOUBLE CLIQUE

Keep It Together, Keiko Carter
DEBBI MICHIKO FLORENCE

SCHOLASTIC and associated logos
are trademarks and/or registered
trademarks of Scholastic Inc.

SCHOLASTIC

scholastic.com/wish

WISHFALL21